PRAISE FOR

Every Other Weekend

A BARNES & NOBLE DISCOVER PICK

"*Every Other Weekend* comes as close as any novel I've read to capturing post-divorce depletion, and Summerfield does so from a child's perspective, which is exactly as gut-wrenching as it sounds. Almost nothing is as sad to witness as a child burnt-out by life—and it is this sensation that lends Summerfield's impressive debut its weight…*Every Other Weekend* manages to be both funny and fierce as it reminds the reader, through Nenny's charming narration, that children are always paying attention."

—Dean Bakopoulos, *New York Times Book Review*

"Summerfield is among the best new writers I've read in a long, long time. In *Every Other Weekend*, she tells the truth but with a beautiful slant, and any reader who comes in contact with this novel will be better for its singular vision."

—Peter Orner, author of *Maggie Brown & Others*

"You are about to meet your new favorite author. Summerfield knows just where the fault lines lie in homes and hearts and families, and in *Every Other Weekend* she leads us to those with a magical compassion. Summerfield's voice is hilarious and scathing and healing. We find ourselves here, inhabitable. In *Every Other Weekend*, Summerfield brings us home."

—Tupelo Hassman, author of *Girlchild*

"*Every Other Weekend* is a sensitive, funny, pitch-perfect tribute to the '80s and that era's loss of innocence, one that speaks with wisdom to the tender complexities of families spliced together in the wake of divorce. By the end of Summerfield's accomplished debut, every character felt like family—or perhaps they just reminded me of my own." —Julie Buntin, author of *Marlena*

"Let this smart, sparkling debut take you back to the '80s and the land of broken homes...A fascinating look at what being a family is really all about." —Kristin Iversen, *Nylon*

"Summerfield creates a sense of time and of place so vivid...Moving but not precious, a gently hopeful novel steeped in late-'80s atmosphere." —*Kirkus Reviews*

"Summerfield's first novel is many things—a nod to late-'80s news and culture, a case study of divided and blended homes, and an imaginative exploration of childhood fears. Mostly, though, it's the beautifully tender story of an eight-year-old's broken heart and her journey toward mending it." —Cortney Ophoff, *Booklist*

"Perceptive...The girl's voice is just right and features an authentically childlike logic...This slice-of-life story moves clearly and confidently." —*Publishers Weekly*

"*Every Other Weekend* is a charming coming-of-age story told from the perspective of Nenny, a slightly neurotic eight-year-old who finds herself splitting time between her dad's run-down apartment and her mom and stepdad's house. I love how Nenny sees and interprets the world and how she makes sense of all the adults dealing with their adult problems. Summerfield captures the bigness of a young kid's everyday life: how everything means so much; how you wish for the parents you think you should have; and how, most of the time, they're not that. I just had a real moment with this book... There's a lovable stray dog, there's a mean nun at Catholic school, and it all takes place in the late '80s. My excitement level for this novel: Liz Lemon high-fiving a million angels."   —Dana Lee, *Book Riot*

"Summerfield captures childhood with incredible tenderness, and this book is absolutely heart-wrenching."

—Gina Mei, *Shondaland*

Every Other Weekend

A Novel

Zulema Renee Summerfield

BACK BAY BOOKS
Little, Brown and Company
New York Boston London

For my family,
and for Theresa

Copyright © 2018 by Zulema Renee Summerfield

Hachette Book Group supports the right to free expression and the value of copyright. The purpose of copyright is to encourage writers and artists to produce the creative works that enrich our culture.

The scanning, uploading, and distribution of this book without permission is a theft of the author's intellectual property. If you would like permission to use material from the book (other than for review purposes), please contact permissions@hbgusa.com. Thank you for your support of the author's rights.

Back Bay Books / Little, Brown and Company
Hachette Book Group
1290 Avenue of the Americas, New York, NY 10104
littlebrown.com

Originally published in hardcover by Little, Brown and Company, April 2018
First Back Bay Books trade paperback edition, September 2019

Back Bay Books is an imprint of Little, Brown and Company, a division of Hachette Book Group, Inc. The Back Bay Books name and logo are trademarks of Hachette Book Group, Inc.

The publisher is not responsible for websites (or their content) that are not owned by the publisher.

The Hachette Speakers Bureau provides a wide range of authors for speaking events. To find out more, go to hachettespeakersbureau.com or call (866) 376-6591.

ISBN 978-0-316-43477-5 (hc) / 978-0-316-43475-1 (pb)
LCCN 2017946211

10 9 8 7 6 5 4 3 2 1

LSC-C

Printed in the United States of America

Every Other Weekend

NENNY LIVES in two houses. The first house is haunted. The second house is not haunted, but still: some nights she lies awake in bed and cannot sleep.

—᠁—

A house is such a thing. A tremendous, monstrous, beautiful thing. Put your face to a window, your ear to a door. See how a house is built—by what darkness, by what light.

House One:
Kensington Drive

How to Stand in
Front of a
Broken Home

NOTE, FIRST, the crepe myrtle. How lovely and silken its wrinkled petals, you might shovel them up like taffeta snow. In spring, scoop fistfuls of petals into sturdy leaf boats, and at dusk, when the neighbors water their lawns and the gutters river up, sail your little crafts downstream, to other cities and children unknown. Have your fun while you can, though, because those petals don't last very long. Soon the myrtle's limbs will be ragged and bare.

It is 1988 and America is full of broken homes. America's time is measured in every-other-weekend-and-sometimes-once-a-week. Her drawers are filled with court papers and photos no one looks at anymore. Her children have bags that're always packed and waiting by the door.

In the driveway, note the brand-new Chevy van. On family trips, scuttle like a bug to get a swivel seat. Yell "Shotgun," punch someone in the arm, cry to Mom if you have to—whatever it takes. If you're not swivelin', you're snivelin', 'cause the back seat reeks of sweat and swarms with ants when summer rolls around. They sneak up the tailpipe and find their way in, a little button of black squirm where someone spilt Hi-C from a can.

—〰—

At Sacred Heart school one day, during Family History Week (which, it turns out, is completely made up), Katie Marion stands at the front of the third-grade classroom, beaming and proud, her family tree clutched to her chest. Something's not right with her drawing. There isn't a single broken branch anywhere. No bandaged grafts, no bark haloed by disease—just two clean branches starting at the top, a grandma branch and a grandpa branch, and then neat smiling non-fissures the whole way down.

"My grandpa met my grandma in 1949," she begins. It's so obvious she's reading off a card taped to the drawing's back. Katie Marion has a stupid mouth. She's happy and nice and her mom brings her hot lunch every day. It's a sin to hate her, which is unfortunate, because Nenny kind of does.

"He was a captain in the air force and she was a secretary on the base. They got married and had three kids: my dad, Uncle Roger, and Aunt Lisa, who died when I was three."

This is said in the same emotional register of everything Katie Marion does or says, except for the time she got stung by a bee. Nenny wants to pencil out her own eye.

"My dad met my mom when he was the principal at this school. He's not the principal anymore. They got married and had my sisters and then me. Mom says don't be surprised if there's another on the way—"

Wait just a pancakin' minute. Hold the ever-lovin' phone. Nenny knows she's not supposed to blurt stuff out, because Sister Timothy will write on her report card "She blurts stuff out," but blurting's what Nenny does.

"Your parents are still *married?*" she blurts. Sister Timothy shoots her a warning glance.

And Katie Marion, stupid Katie Marion, she just blinks her big no-sin eyes.

"Well, sure," she says. "Aren't yours?"

(Pencil stab.)

"Yeah," Nenny finally says, offering a dramatic pause. "But not to each other."

It only takes a second before everyone figures out that this is the funniest thing they've ever heard. The whole room erupts in laughter, and everyone's clapping and slapping their knees—everyone except Sister Timothy, who yells "Go to the office!" as she thrusts the hall pass into Nenny's hands.

A bright wave of laughter follows her, hot sizzling relief that someone said what they were all thinking. Katie Marion stands dumbstruck still, as surprised as if someone's told her that God doesn't exist or wishes don't actually come true. Katie Marion's an idiot, that's for sure, but it isn't her fault. Idiocy is genetic—just look at her stupid family tree. Besides, there's grace inside Nenny somewhere. She could probably trace its source, if someone would only show her how. Grace to forgive, grace to excuse, grace to turn a thousand blind eyes. A grace simple enough to flash Katie Marion a quiet look as Nenny leaves.

Come on over to Kensington Drive. Stand outside of my house anytime.

A Brief History of
Why Everything Sucks

EARLY LAST year Nenny's parents called the kids in for dinner, served them each a plate of macaroni and cheese, turned the TV off, and announced that they were getting a divorce. Tiny didn't know what that meant, so Dad took a deep breath and explained. "Your mom and I aren't going to live together anymore," and to Nenny that made sense, because it was clear they were miserable, and Bubbles seemed fine with it too, because he was the oldest and could roll with anything—but Tiny? Poor Tiny? He just collapsed in a ball on the floor and cried. When he did that, Mom couldn't help it: she started crying too. Bubbles slid off his chair and started to go somewhere but then stopped, standing by the table looking terribly confused. Finally Dad said, "All right, let's clean up," in a voice so sad and distant that Nenny knew for the first time what forever meant, and knew that it wasn't good.

—⁂—

Within a matter of weeks, it seemed, everything changed. They sold the house in Yucaipa and Dad went to live in an apartment while Mom moved into a two-bedroom house with a woman named Corinne, who was another nurse at the hospital. Sometimes, when Mom was gone at work, Corinne took them to the orange grove at the end of the street. Someone had hung a tire swing. The grove was mysterious in a prehistoric kind of way. Shadows turned bluish and soft once you stepped in, and likely there were dead things there.

A strange mechanical ritual emerged: Mom went to work, the three of them ducked into the grove with Corinne, and then Tiny would swing, and then Nenny, and then Bubbles, and then Tiny again. While you waited for your turn you sat in the dirt and picked at your shoes, pushing sticks through the eyelets, unraveling the laces, until it was your turn again, and then Corinne would push you, quiet and gentle and slow. It was like slipping into a dream no one'd had before.

Corinne never tried to console them about the divorce and the change in their lives. For this, Nenny loved her.

And then Dad would show up, every other weekend and one night a week, looking like someone had blown him up and had left a weird, featureless man in his place. On Wednesdays he'd take them to McDonald's and they'd eat in silence, and every other Friday he'd pick them up for weekends at his house. They were long weekends, dull and quiet in a sad, sort of lonely way.

—ɯ—

Soon Rick came along. He worked at the hospital with Mom too. He was bald as a cue and was very no-nonsense. Rick had been in Vietnam.

Rick had two kids, Charles and Kat. Charles was skinny as a bean and, like Nenny, was about to enter third grade. Kat was sixteen. It didn't matter what you said to her, she'd just snort and roll her eyes. Mom took Nenny and the boys to Rick's every couple of days, where they watched Charles run around with sticks while Kat ignored them all, reading *Seventeen* in the shade. On the upside, Rick did have a pool—though more often than not swimming was just Charles doing cannonballs while Nenny and the boys stuck timidly to the sides.

Eventually Mom and Rick would emerge from the dark of the house looking rumpled and unkempt, and then they'd all eat pizza or Chinese food around a table that was far too small for seven people, while Rick's cat eyed everyone suspiciously from the corner of the room. One day in June, Mom made an announcement: "Kids, we're moving in!" Like this was somehow good news, like it made a whole ton of sense. What about the tire swing? Does Dad even know his way here?

So that's how it is: Mom and Rick got married and Nenny's got a new family and they've all got adjustments to make. That's what Rick keeps saying, as if the fact that this sucks for everyone should make them all feel better.

Turns out, Dad does know his way here. Except that when he shows up now, he doesn't even come to the door. He just sits in the car, staring straight ahead, honking.

Diminishing the Power

LITTLE NENNY has always been a nervous nelly. She was born with a natural predilection for alarm. Whatever can go wrong, will go wrong. This simple irrationality governs her whole life—top to bottom, inside and out.

Knock-kneed and a little stormy-eyed, she is far too small for the thoughts that haunt her. Do they contain her or does she contain them? If the heart is a receptacle, a little bin where all your troubles go, then Nenny's overflows to the point of being overwhelmed.

Someone will leave the stove on and the house will burn to the ground. She'll trip and break her neck on the stairs. She'll go swimming and her foot will get caught in the drain at the bottom of the pool (she saw this once on TV). The house will fill with gas and no one will smell it and they'll all just go about their business, la dee da, and then some idiot will come over and light a match and blow them all to smithereens. It's going to happen because it's happened before, to one of Kat's friends who moved away to Michigan. Cross her heart and hope to die—except that's the problem. She doesn't want to die. Nenny doesn't want to die at all.

You could make a catalog of these fears and sell it for a pretty penny. Give it a nice shiny cover with a drawing of a girl trembling and sweating and with her fingers crammed in her mouth. Call it something like *When a Child Suffers the Inevitability of Doom*.

Every Thursday night, Mom puts Nenny to bed. It can only be once a week because Mom works late, and also there are so many people in this stupid house and not enough Mom to go around. She sits on the edge of Nenny's bed and takes Nenny's hand in her own, pets it like it's a dying hamster, and she takes a deep breath and tells Nenny to take a deep breath too, and they breathe in all the breath they've got and their chests expand like too-full balloons, and they exhale—*whoooooooo*—and Mom tilts her head and half smiles, half frowns with a look that means it's time to get real, and she stops petting but still holds Nenny's hand and says, "What's been on your mind?"

"Everything," Nenny says, because it's true. It's always true.

"Everything is on your mind?" she asks, and Nenny nods. "Everything is on your mind." Mom makes this simple reaffirmation, then lets a quiet pause fill the room. She's good at this, at stopping just long enough to let whatever you said float around, long enough to collect meaning but not long enough to gather dust. She is a nurse, after all.

"And how does that feel? To have everything on your mind?"

Part of Nenny hates stupid questions, wishes she could swipe all stupid questions off the face of the earth. But the other part of her, the more important, lasting part, would give everything to spend the rest of eternity in a half-dark room with Mom's soft voice swirling around. Sister Timothy would send her to hell just for thinking it, but Nenny doesn't care: she'd give her very soul.

"It feels bad," Nenny says. "Really bad."

"Okay. Where does it feel bad? Does it feel bad in your head? In your stomach? Can you point to where it feels bad?"

This whole thing—the breathing, the check-ins, locating the bad—they recently learned from Uncle Max, who is Rick's brother and a counselor at a school for troubled boys. When you're feeling something, find the place where you're feeling it the most. It's sometimes in your chest, sometimes in your head, often in your stomach, rarely in your toes. Once you've found it, close your eyes and imagine it gone. It's called "diminishing the power." It sounds easier than it is. They've been diminishing the power for months now, since the earthquake in July and Nenny's freak-out: crying, puking, pulling out her hair.

"Is it here?" Mom says and points to her own head. "Here?" Her stomach. "Here?" Her heart. But Nenny doesn't say anything now, and Nenny doesn't point.

There aren't enough fingers to point with.

FEAR #18: DROUGHT

THEY'RE TALKING about drought on TV and then it happens—the whole world runs suddenly dry. Tiny's brushing his teeth and Nenny's shouting, "Turn the faucet off when you brush!" but he refuses because he's a jerk and he never listens to anything Nenny has to say even though the *whole existence of everything* depends on it—and then *schlp!* The water's gone.

The water's gone! They run to all the faucets in the house but none of them work, so they race outside to check the hose but the hose is useless, and they look at the grass and the grass shrivels up, and they turn to the flowers and the flowers shrivel up, and then the trees all shrivel up too, and Nenny shouts, "The pool!" because it's their last resort even though everyone knows that if you drink pool water you'll throw up everywhere and then poop in your pants.

Doesn't matter, because the pool's now dried up too.

They look to the sky then, and the clouds, terribly, begin to disappear. The clouds suck in and pucker up like an old lady's face when she sleeps, collapse like little universes turning in on themselves before they finally evaporate, gone.

"Look what you did, dummy," Nenny says. But when she turns to Tiny, there's no Tiny anymore—just a pile of smoking and parched and dried-up Tiny clothes.

Before

Who knows why things fall apart, or why some things happen and others don't, or why two people who loved each other once don't love each other anymore. Nenny could speculate all night about Mom and Dad's marriage or Mom and Dad's divorce, and sometimes she does. She doesn't exactly want to or intend to, but her brain does funny things when she cannot sleep—and often she cannot sleep.

The break wasn't all that long ago but seems far away in time. They lived in Yucaipa then, which is a rock-strewn and lonely place, and the family across the street were hunchbacks—mama hunchback, papa hunchback, two hunchback boys. The yard next door was littered with trash, and their own yard was all rocks and no grass. There was hardly any furniture in that Yucaipa house. Everyone had a bed and there was a table with chairs, but when they watched TV, they sat on the floor. Mom worked the night shift at the hospital, gone from dusk until dawn, and at night Nenny stood in bed, her face at the window, waiting for Mom to come home, and some nights—most nights—she cried. Thinking about that house now—late on a

Saturday, in her sleeping bag on Dad's floor—even all these months later, it still makes her stomach ache.

Maybe in other houses divorce comes banging loud like drums, but not at the house in Yucaipa. It just seemed like after a while Mom and Dad didn't talk anymore; they'd pass by each other in the house, wordlessly, the way people who don't know each other do. Some days Mom wasn't around at all, and Dad said she was working, but Nenny knew that probably wasn't true.

Once they walked down to Taco Bell for lunch, on one of those days Mom should have been at home but wasn't. It was too hot to be walking, but Mom had the car. Dad ordered four burritos, the kind that cost only thirty-five cents, and they ate in a booth near the back. They were the only people there. Halfway home, Nenny realized she'd forgotten her doll, back on the bench in the corner booth. It was a floppy little thing, a sack of loose limbs with a plastic face, nothing like a real baby. Still, she didn't want to be without it.

"What do you mean you forgot? Where is it?" They were at the stoplight, cars whizzing past, Dad's hair wild in the sweltering wind.

"I guess back at the booth," Nenny said weakly. She had to stare at the sidewalk, at her shoes, otherwise she'd cry.

"Dammit, Nenny." Dad's face was splotched with rage. "I told you to leave it at home." Which was true, he did, but she'd begged. "Dammit," he said again. Dad had cursed before but never at Nenny or the boys. He started to march back, Nenny and the boys trailing behind, silent in the way when one of you is in trouble so all of you are but really no one is. Even then, young as they were, they knew it wasn't about the heat or the walk back to Taco Bell. They knew it wasn't about them at all.

Space Rocks

IT'S MONDAY and they're walking to school, Nenny and the boys and Charles. Kat takes the bus to public high school, which pisses her off because she wants to learn how to drive. Is it strange that they go to private school? Probably. Nenny doubts Rick believes in God, and Mom prays but never goes to church. Dad takes them to church on Sundays but sporadically, maybe like once a month. Nenny wonders if school was somehow a condition of the divorce, the only demand of Dad's: *If you're going to raise my kids in a godless house, they'll at least go to Catholic school.* It's hard to say. What Nenny does know is that in August, when Mom and Rick told Charles he'd be joining Nenny and the boys, he flipped his lid. "What the crap! With those freaks?!" as if Nenny and the boys were another species, as if they weren't sitting right there. Rick said, "That's enough," discussion over. And though it made little sense—Why would Rick pay for Charles to go to school? He hates spending money—and Rick seems hard as nails, at the end of the day he wasn't going to let Charles call them freaks, and that felt noteworthy in some regard.

Charles walks ahead of them now, as always. He kicks pebbles off the sidewalk and makes rude faces at passing cars. He acts like he doesn't need any of this, like he could leave at the drop of a hat and go live with his mom if he really wanted to, have his pick of houses and lives—though everyone knows that's not really true.

"Let's pretend it's space rocks," Tiny calls to Charles.

"Let's not and say we did," Charles says, not even turning around.

"But they was space rocks last week," Tiny protests. Last week Tiny'd suggested they have an adventure out in space, and Charles had been game. He ran ahead and ducked behind trees, shot his space laser twig, and shouted, "Kill the alien bastards!" And though he'd clearly usurped Tiny's game—kind of did his own thing, running around chucking rocks over fences and into the street—it didn't matter. Tiny loved it. He talked about it for two whole days.

"Last week's over," Charles says and spits in the grass. He and Kat went to their mom's this weekend, and Tiny's just entered kindergarten so he doesn't get it yet: how fast things can turn, that a lot can change in two days.

"But—"

"Shut up about it, already," Charles says. Tiny tucks his chin and looks like he might cry.

Bubbles doesn't say anything, doesn't even glance up, just keeps his eyes on his feet. He's the oldest after Kat, almost eleven, but even so, he's surprisingly meek. He stays on the sidelines, allowing himself to be swallowed into the background of whatever is going on. Nenny feels a sudden spark of rage, wants to shake Bubbles angry and awake. *Do something, for criminy's sake. He's your little brother. Defend him, you goon.*

"Give it to me," she says. She puts her hand out for the rock because she can't stand it anymore, Charles and Bubbles being so hopelessly cruel. Yes, Tiny is annoying as hell, but he's just a kid. They call him Tiny for a reason.

Still: she waits a good minute until the other two have walked away.

"Okay, where are we again?"

"The moon!"

"All right. And who am I again?"

"Manny Hernandez!"

Nenny rolls her eyes. "Okay. And I eat them?" She doesn't really remember the plot to Friday's game because, Tiny-constructed, it made no sense.

"Yeah, an' when you eat 'em a alien comes from the rock an' eats your brain so then you have to walk funny, like this"—he twitches his arm and drags his foot—"an' then I shoot you to set Manny free. Okay?"

"Okay," she says and goes *"Nom, nom"* until Tiny laughs. Sometimes—she can't help it—Nenny plays her own pretend game, though she would never tell anyone about it, not in a million years. Late at night when she can't sleep, or in the earliest hours before the alarm, she imagines them all in a room, including Dad, sitting in a circle like musical chairs. She knows it's foolish; she knows this fantasy makes no sense. But there it is, everything slowing for a bit and everyone just being who they really are. But it's stupid—it's like wishing for a pot of gold when there hasn't even been rain.

When they get to school, they all go their separate ways. She watches Charles throw his backpack at Dalton Mulligan, a tall kid with freckles in the other third grade. She wonders if Dalton is Charles's friend, what it's like to be friends with Charles. On the first day of school Yvonne Peralta pointed to Charles across the yard and said, "Is that your new brother?" Nenny didn't answer right away. At home he talks to Nenny and the boys or does not talk to them, either hands Tiny or Bubbles a Nintendo controller and lets them play or else says "Go away." He's inconsistent, pushing them out or letting them in depending on his mood. And everyone knows that when someone shuts you out, you only want them more. Finally Yvonne poked Nenny's ribs, like *Hey, hello,* and Nenny said, "I guess so," which was not the most assertive of answers but was closest to the truth. You cannot claim that which does not want to be owned.

A Weekend at Dad's

HAVING DIVORCED parents is like living in one of those claw machines at the pizza parlor: you're just hanging around, minding your own business, and then every other weekend you get plucked up and flung somewhere else. Except it's less fun than the pizza place. It's not like Nenny ever thinks *Yippee, a weekend at Dad's.*

Every other Friday, Dad's Pinto chugs into the parking lot at school. It smells like coffee and Old Spice cologne, and has dents in its sides and scratches on the doors because he doesn't exactly pay close attention when he drives. There's trash everywhere and stains on the seats, not because he's a slob but because he doesn't remember to be tidy, and those are two different things. A slob is someone who doesn't care; Dad is someone who forgets to care. Today he honks the horn and waves when he sees them, even gets out to open doors and clear papers and folders off the seats.

"Get in! Get in!" he says.

"Daddy," Tiny starts in right away, "did you know a cheetah is the fastest aminal in the world?" He fits himself right into

Dad's good mood, but Nenny's a little suspicious. She's seen these moods hundreds of times and knows they don't really last.

"You don't say?" Dad says, poking at the radio buttons. "Hey, is anybody hungry?"

"I'm hungry," Tiny says.

"I could eat," Bubbles says.

"And what about my favorite daughter?" Dad says, glancing back. It's a familiar joke—she's his *only* daughter—but Nenny feels her face flush anyways.

"To Mickey D's?" Dad says, and Tiny cheers. Dad goes, "Whoop, got your nose!" and swipes playfully at Tiny's face. Tiny laughs and laughs, though that's an old joke too.

—⁓—

"You know what? I think today we'll take it to go," Dad says when the girl at the counter asks. "Let's go to the park."

"But I want to play in the ball room," Tiny whines.

"Play till the food comes," Dad says, then to Bubbles, "Go with your brother."

Nenny and Dad sit in a booth while they wait for their order. Nenny takes the wrapper off a straw, smooshes it into a ball. Dad taps his key on the Formica, watching people come and go, then blinks and turns to her with a smile, remembering she's there.

"Okay," he says definitively, like picking up where they'd left off—which is nowhere. "What're they teaching you guys?"

He means in history. "We're learning about the Egyptians," she says.

"The Egyptians, huh?" His eyes light up. "King Tut!" he

sings, his voice lowered an octave, but Nenny just smiles tautly. She doesn't know that song.

"That's Steve Martin," he says, a bit reproachfully, but sees that she has no idea what he's talking about. He waves it off. "Anyway. Okay. So, the Egyptians. You learning hieroglyphics?"

"Yeah." Somehow it's almost harder to relax when he's in a good mood. There's more pressure to keep it up, keep it going. "We're learning about mummies." Just then the girl comes by with their bag, which truthfully is something of a relief.

It's a beautiful day. The trees are rainbowed with early fall leaves and there are lots of other people at the park. Everyone seems happy. "Let's eat by the lake," Dad says and remembers their coats and doesn't lock the keys in the car. He sings, "King Tut!" as they walk, and when some guy throws a football and the football rolls to Dad's feet, he picks it up and throws it back. For a brief moment it seems possible that his mood actually *will* last. Nenny thinks, *Maybe this is him*, the dad she's been waiting for since the divorce, since before that even, attentive and silly and sweet, that maybe her real dad is back or has finally arrived.

Which is, of course, totally foolish, because the minute they get to the lake Dad shouts, "God dam*mit!*"

"Daddy, what happened?" Tiny says, but then they see what the fuss is about: Dad's stepped in a giant dog turd.

"Dammit," he says again.

"It's okay," Bubbles says, like a parent would, grabbing a stick. "You can scrape it off."

"Don't touch it!" Dad yells, which is weird because Bubbles wasn't. "Ugh. *Ugh*," he keeps saying, and they watch for a minute as Dad—McDonald's bag in hand, glasses sliding down his nose, Banning Unified ID swinging against his chest— grumbles in disgust and drags his foot across the grass. Nenny knew his mood wouldn't endure but had no idea it would end with dog poop. It's almost funny, though Nenny and the boys are smart enough not to laugh.

"Just everyone sit down," Dad finally says, and they sit at the picnic table. He irritably hands out the food and they start to eat.

Nenny's burger is smeared with ketchup and she practically gags, but she knows better than to complain. Also, today's Happy Meal toy is a puzzle, which is not a toy. After a while Tiny says, "Can I go play?" He has to ask twice before Dad nods. Dad doesn't tell Bubbles to go with him, but Bubbles stands up anyways, laying a hand on his shoulder before he goes. "Don't worry, Dad," he says. "It's just some poop."

Nenny looks at Dad, who doesn't seem to notice she's still there. He takes a dejected bite of his Big Mac, then lets it kind of flop onto the wrapper and stares at the ground while he chews. An hour ago he seemed ready for anything—peppy, funny, father of the year. Now he just looks sad, and there are wrinkles in his coat and a coffee stain on his tie she hadn't noticed before. It doesn't seem fair, any of it: Mom got a new house and a new family, and Dad got what? A crappy apartment with a gross pool? Like, who does Dad even talk to? Does he have any friends?

"Daddy, there's tadpoles in here," Tiny calls from the lake's edge.

"A whole bunch," Bubbles echoes, but Dad just says, "Let's go," and leaves it to Nenny to gather the trash. He stops every ten feet or so on the way to the car, grunting and swiping his shoe across the grass. Even then, despite all that, despite his efforts, the whole ride home smells distinctly like turd.

Discord

IT'S LATE afternoon, and Nenny and Charles and the boys are doing homework at the table while Mom cooks, when suddenly Kat comes thundering down the stairs. She's clutching a stick of Teen Secret in her hand. "Who did this?" she demands. No one knows what she's talking about. She starts waving the deodorant around. "I *said*, who *did* this?" All she gets are blank stares.

"Who did what, Kat?" Mom says, but instead of answering, Kat storms back upstairs. Of course they all follow her, except Mom, who just sighs. They scramble and shove past one another up the steps, and Kat's already in the bathroom when they arrive, fuming by the towel rack. They crowd the doorway, poking their heads in to see.

"Someone," she says, her voice like sliced metal, "smeared my deodorant all over the hamper and *ruined* it." They look down at the hamper. Sure enough, it's covered in a thick layer of white paste.

"That was me," Tiny says, as if just now clueing in to what she's talking about. "I did that."

Kat looks at him, seething. "You'd better replace my deodorant!"

"I don't have any money!" Tiny cries.

"You'd better find some money, *today*."

It's the most ridiculous argument that's ever been had, this week anyways. Charles smacks Tiny on the head, then runs downstairs, the boys close behind. "Your brother's a creep," Kat says to Nenny, as if this is somehow her fault. Nenny wants to say *So is yours*, because yesterday Bubbles fell asleep on the couch and Charles woke him up by dragging a dirty sock across his face. But she doesn't say it, because she wants to be in Kat's good graces, and besides, what's the point?

Back downstairs, Mom's sitting with Tiny at the table. "Honey, why did you smear the hamper like that?"

"I was tryin' to poop and it wouldn't come out and I got bored," Tiny says, already coloring again, as if smearing deodorant across a hamper is the most ordinary thing in the world.

Mom blinks a little and shakes her head. "Well, you need to apologize. Kat is very upset."

"You're damn straight I'm upset," Kat yells from the top of the stairs.

"I know! I'll make her a cod," Tiny whispers, already folding a piece of paper.

"I think that's a great idea," Mom says, though it's clear she knows it won't accomplish much.

The card has one of his boxy people drawn on it, purple with seven-finger hands, holding what looks like a balloon. He puts it on the bathroom counter, along with a pile of coins, about thirty-five cents. When Kat comes down later, he looks at her brightly. "Did you get my cod?"

"*Yes*, I got your stupid card," Kat says, and Mom looks at her like *Cool it, he's only six*. "Just stay the hell away from my stuff." She stomps back upstairs.

"Okay!" he chirps, then runs to play in the other room.

When Rick gets home, Mom explains the whole thing. "I guess he was pooping and the deodorant was on the counter? Who knows."

"Does it still work?" Rick asks, emptying his lunch sack.

"Does what still work?"

"The hamper. Does it still hold clothes?"

"Well, yeah, it still holds clothes."

"All right, then," he says, as if not having to replace the hamper is what matters. He goes upstairs to change out of his scrubs, and Nenny can tell Mom is frustrated, because when she catches Nenny watching, she smiles tightly before turning back to the stove.

Truthfully? Nenny has no idea why Mom loves Rick. He hardly ever laughs, and he's usually in a sort of crappy mood—not like being grumpy but right beside grumpy, like he might step into grumpy at any time. He's not ugly but he isn't exactly handsome, unless you can be handsome and also be bald. In their wedding photos they look joyful enough—smiling together on some courthouse steps—but who knows. They went off and got married in Las Vegas one weekend when Kat and Charles were at their mom's and Nenny and the boys were at Dad's. Which Nenny wasn't happy about either; it's like they kept it to themselves on purpose, and it didn't even occur to them that the kids should be invited and that Nenny should be the flower girl.

Anyway, maybe that's why Rick's so grumbly all the time. This probably isn't exactly what he bargained for. But then again, who did?

Gramma B

GRAMMA B, with her breasts like swinging sacks of grain. When she walks, it's like watching Big Ben toll. Gramma B lives in a single-wide off San Bernardino Avenue, where women in tiny skirts and high heels stroll lonesome as ghosts in the night. She chain-smokes mentholated Kools and spends her time with bingo and crochet.

Nenny doesn't know what the *B* stands for.

Gramma B is Rick's mom. She doesn't talk much, and her eyes look swallowed in her face. There'd been a hardscrabble life years ago, rumbling around from motels to farmstead posts all across the northern New Mexico plains—but by the time Nenny knows her, it's just a lot of doilies and awkward standing around.

"Did you get a new blender?" Rick asks, practically yells, because there's something the matter with her ears.

"Yeahp. Mine was bust." She starts to wave a hand toward the kitchen but then stops, as if realizing it's the most boring thing in the world, which it is. Outside, the boys chase lizards and Kat flirts with guys who live in the trailer park, but it's too

hot out there and besides: Gramma B's got an extensive collection of tiny animal figurines. Also, a stuffed parrot and a dog
named Nuisance.

Here's a thing that Nenny will never admit, not to anyone,
ever: one afternoon, the sun slicing slantwise through the curtains and lighting up the lace, just a few weeks after Gramma
B got her stage four diagnosis ("It won't be long now," the doctor said), Nenny stands before the glass shelves of figurines and
wonders which will be hers when Gramma B dies. It is awful
and wonderful at once. It's like having something sparkling but
grey sloshing around in her guts.

"B?" Mom shouts. "I think you should take some of these!"
She's waving a bottle of vitamins near Gramma B's face, and
Gramma's nodding but also squinting and batting at the air like
it's swarming with flies. Rick keeps picking stuff up and putting
it down, picking it up and putting it down. Supposedly the parrot could talk. Dirty words like a sailor, "When the Moon Hits
Your Eye," things like that. Won three state fair ribbons for that
song before he died, Gramma B likes to say. Now he sits stiff and
stuffed on a perch in a cage. Dulled green feathers, beady glass
eyes. Nuisance, who never does anything, who doesn't make any
noise or cause any trouble and who can't even be bothered to
play, sleeps like a rock, snoring under the parrot's cage by the
door.

Nuisance

ON THE drive home, Mom says, "Nuisance? Who names a dog Nuisance?" She forces a small laugh and looks over at Rick.

But Rick is just driving. Even the kids know to shut the hell up.

It won't be long now. Nenny watches the women on San Bernardino Avenue.

Fashions

To LIVE in two houses is to have your feet planted precariously in two separate worlds. Mom's house is a chaos of frenzy and needs and noise. Someone's always running up or down the stairs, someone screams at someone else, video games blast, Kat yammers on the phone, Tiny blathers on about who knows what, Charles flip-flops between rowdy and detached, Bubbles often seems confused. Mom toggles back and forth between saintly and irritated, like putting food coloring in the milk just for fun but then yelling "No feet on the goddamned couch!" Rick is humorless and has bizarre, inflexible rules: no reading on the toilet, cabinets and drawers have to be closed. The cat pukes hair balls the size of other cats, and there's always a fight about who has to clean it up. The upstairs bathroom stinks like hair spray and boy pee; everyone is testy and irritable and annoyed. If it seems that their collective frustration and disappointment should unite them, it doesn't. It only pushes them further apart, like debris kicked up by a storm. In the evenings, when dinner's ready, Rick doesn't waste his time wandering the house to find them all, just puts two fingers in his mouth and whistles from the bottom of the stairs. He hates to spend money, so they hardly ever go out to eat.

At Dad's, though, they eat out all the time. Denny's and McDonald's and Carl's Jr. and Jack in the Box. At home in the apartment, they eat chips and cookies and crackers from paper plates, keep their clothes in small suitcases, sleep in sleeping bags on the floor. In the months after the divorce, when Mom moved in with Rick, there was a mania about Dad that's hard to explain. It was like watching someone lose their mind. He'd pick them up for a weekend of camping, even if the forecast wasn't good. "Come out of the tent, guys! This is nature!" he'd call, pointlessly chopping wood in the rain. He'd take them to a movie, then say, "Let's see another!" or to 31 Flavors and encourage them to "Go on, try them all!" But other weekends he'd put on *Metropolis* to bore them while he slept like a dead man on the couch in the middle of the day. Once Bubbles said, "He's just trying to be a dad." He didn't say "good dad" or "better dad," and Nenny didn't ask.

But it's been close to four months, and things have settled in their own way. They don't really watch *Metropolis* anymore.

—␣␣—

The nice thing about weekends at Dad's is that Boots lives right down the hall. Everyone calls her Boots because it rhymes with "Oots," which is a derivation of her last name. Boots goes to public school and lives with her mother in an apartment filled with plants and colorful paintings on the walls. She wears cropped neon-colored shirts stamped with animal prints and acid-washed jeans that she makes herself in the building's yard. She seems older than Nenny, but they're the same age, and

Nenny likes her because she's nice and will talk about whatever and does interesting things, unlike all the dorks at Sacred Heart. All they want to do is play jump rope and braid each other's hair.

It's a Saturday in fall, and crows rustle and squawk in the trees. There are cones around the pool because supposedly it's getting cleaned, so all the other apartment kids are playing behind the building in the parking lot. It's better this way, talking to Boots without a bunch of babies hanging around.

"You wanna draw fashions?" Boots asks.

"Sure," Nenny says. It's Boots's favorite thing to do, and Nenny's learned a lot about fashion in the past few months, designing clothes with Boots. If you're going to mix patterns, mix at least three—stripes *with* chevrons *with* plaid, for example. Always incorporate neon, the brighter the better. Never wear navy with black. Remember: layer, layer, layer. It's the kind of stuff that doesn't occur to you when you wear a uniform to school.

"Okay." Boots starts pulling markers and pens from her backpack. She regularly carries art supplies. "What's our theme?" When they draw fashions, they always have a theme.

"Um, let me think." Nenny looks out over the concrete and the murky pool. Last time it was ball gowns, and winter wear the time before that—hot new takes on coats and scarves. "How about school uniforms?"

Boots pops her eyes. "That is brilliant," she says, laying notebooks down. "We'll reinvent your entire wardrobe."

They start to draw, both girls fixated on their task. Boots doodles some blazers with matching ties, then reworks the saddle shoe. Nenny sketches variations on the white blouse. When Boots designs a new skirt, this one short and inches above the knee, Nenny says, "No way. Mother Superior would flip."

There's a jumper with shoulder pads, then one with a bold sash. Plaid is replaced with paint splatters and polka dots. They discuss the importance of accessorizing, all the cool things you could do with bleach. The afternoon wears pleasantly on.

"Do you like wearing a uniform?" Boots asks.

Nenny wrinkles her nose. "Not really. It's too hot when it's hot and too cold when it's cold." She thinks. "Also, they itch."

"What're they made of? Like, what's the cloth?" It's the kind of question Boots would ask. She's curious about most things.

"I don't know. Sand?" And Boots smiles and bugs her eyes again. She buries her head for a quick sketch, then turns her paper toward Nenny. "Look at this," she says. She's drawn a hill of sand with a girl's head popping out, and the girl looks a lot like Nenny. They both laugh.

It's nice here, it's simple—no drama, nothing's a big deal. Nenny likes being with Boots because it's easy in a way that being at home is not. It feels straightforward and therefore real.

"Wanna walk to Thrifty's?" Boots asks.

"Sure," Nenny says, so they do.

FEAR #37: EARTHQUAKE

A NINE point five is going to strike and rip the town, their street, their house, *them,* in two. What starts as a soft rumble in the middle of the night swiftly transforms into the apocalyptic shrieking of the earth itself, like God howling as a beast would howl and then tearing off his clothes. The bunk beds buckle and Tiny is crushed like a pancake. Kat is ripped to shreds by broken glass. Bubbles, scrambling for the safety of an open doorway, is struck in the head by a falling beam, and his brain goes *pop!* out of his skull. Charles—not one to panic, but still, his decisions are never wise—somehow ends up in the pool, and dies when a live wire snakes across the ground and lands in the shallow end, and he is zapped so bad that his hair turns white and his eyeballs explode and his spine comes shooting, strangely, out of his chest. He never stands a chance.

Thankfully, Mom and Rick die peacefully in their sleep.

Nenny, however, gets trapped in a tiny airtight crevice when two walls collapse, her face smashed into her knees and drywall smooshing her spine. For a few days—after the initial, high-pitched panic—she is fine. She befriends a small field mouse that has made its way inside a crack, and passes the time telling him stories about his own magic-filled and adventurous youth: "And you were proclaimed a knight, and all the other mice children cheered!" She names the mouse BobbySocks, and on some deep, unarticulated, spiritual level—where everything glows and nothing has a name—she is sure that this is all somehow meant to be: a shuddering earth led to this collapsed wall led to this entrapment led to this fated friendship between rodent and girl. An epic, transformative epiphany is about to occur, when BobbySocks begins to nibble her toe.

That's how Nenny dies: not by succumbing to starvation and fatigue, but by being eaten alive.

Sorority

LIKE MOST girls her age, Nenny has always wanted a sister. Someone to share secrets with, a guide for life's adventures, a mentor for things like bras and maxi pads and what to do about boys. She's long dreamt of a sisterhood like Mallory and Jennifer Keaton's on *Family Ties*. It's sometimes biting and a little mean, okay—but they always come back to each other. They always circle back to love.

Kat, to be sure, is *not* what Nenny had in mind. None of this is what Nenny had in mind. They share the biggest room in the house, but still it's too small, crowded with Kat's posters and knickknacks. Her bed is never made; her dresser vomits clothes. She hardly talks to Nenny, and when she does, it's only to say something crass or rude. "You know Jordan Knight is gay, right?" Kat with her crimped hair and mismatched earrings and lip gloss and Guess jeans. She listens to bands like Mötley Crüe and Poison, is obsessed with Bret Michaels, runs her fingers over his face in some magazine and purrs "Bret is such a babe" to whoever's on the phone, seems not to notice or care that he looks like a girl. Kat wears blue eye shadow and lacquers her hair with Aqua Net and goes on dates with boys no one ever meets because "I'd rather *die*" than invite them in. Mom says things like "They should at least come to the door" and Rick says, "Leave it alone," because it's better to surrender some battles than to wage all-out war. So Kat puts on earrings that nearly reach her chin, props a magazine next to the mirror and follows the steps for lipstick and liner and blush—the "perfect sun-kissed look"—listens to "Unskinny Bop" once, then twice, then again, puts on a pair of pink socks and over those a pair of neon green, steps into her white pumps, and it's been almost four months now, four months crammed together in the world's smallest room, and Nenny knows better than to ask where Kat is going, knows that at best she'll be told to "mind your own beeswax" and at worst she'll be ignored. Nenny looks through the window down to where Kat stands at the bottom of the drive, a purse slung over her shoulder and snapping her gum, waiting for this week's dream date to come and rescue her, to come and whisk her away.

Bizarre Beginnings

THE WAY Mom tells it is that one day last week, while she was filling up gas, the dog just jumped into the back seat and would not budge. She had no choice but to bring it home. What doesn't make sense to Nenny is, why was the back door of the car hanging wide open? Who opens the *back* door when they go to fill up gas? It just doesn't add up—but terrible stories have bizarre beginnings, so somehow the whole thing fits.

Anyway, now they have a dog. She's filthy as all get-out and not technically mangy but mangy still. She looks as though the devil poured grease on her fur before he ran away laughing. Her eyes too: there's something wrong with her eyes. One's always swelling up and glazing over, and a yolk-yellow ooze drips out of both. But she's okay—she doesn't bark much and doesn't bother them while they eat.

After about four days, the kids realize she doesn't have a name. "Hey! What should we call the dog?" someone says when they're watching TV. They look at one another, then at the dog, then back at one another, and their eyes start to wander the room. It's the visual equivalent of grasping at straws, because they really don't know the dog well enough to have a whole list of potential names. They could call her Fleabag or Mange, but that doesn't seem right. So everyone's looking around during commercials — commercials don't matter anyway.

"How about ... Rex?" Bubbles says.

"Rex is a boy's name, stupid," Charles says.

"So?"

"So she's a girl."

"Ooh! I know! Thursday! Cause today is —"

"How about Kat?" Nenny says, and everyone laughs because Kat's not there.

"Um ... Lampy?" Bubbles tries again.

"*Lamp*y?"

"Yeah. Like the lamp."

"How about Daisy?" Charles suggests.

"Daisy don't work," Tiny says.

"Why in the hell not?"

"Cause daisies are yellow, and this dog is ... mud."

"Sh! It's back!"

A silence befalls them that's nearly religious because this is, after all, TV. There's trouble in the Huxtable house. Denise is upset because the record company where she works won't promote her (it's been three whole weeks!) and Cliff's gotta have a physical because he eats way too many hoagies and trea—

"How 'bout Cosby?" Tiny shouts in the middle of the show, and they're just about to riot and start tearing off ears when they realize: it's actually a pretty good name. Nenny doesn't point out that it's also kind of a boy name—at least that's the way it sounds—'cause she knows it's better than nothing. Certainly it's better than Lampy.

So that's how Cosby gets her name.

—⚹—

Cosby is a decent, if mellow, family dog. She likes to lie around while they watch TV, and seems relieved and grateful when they feed her every night. It's clear she didn't get fed much, or at least not with any kind of consistency, by whoever owned her before. She wolfs the whole bowl of bits down and hardly even chews, as if each is her last and only meal. One afternoon, Charles goes out to find something in the garage, and at one point he picks up a baseball bat to move it to the side. When he does, Cosby—silent lump of a dog, never barks, never complains—scurries under the parked car, trembling and whimpering, and cannot be coaxed out all day. Rick becomes suspicious. Two days later, Rick tries it again: picks up a baseball bat and just holds it in his hand. Same thing: she curls under the car and whines. Afterward, Rick is very quiet, so they press him—"What? What is it?"—until he solemnly explains: Cosby had been abused.

Some things are impossible to fathom. That rage or spite or drunken blindness or whatever it is, whatever you call it, could compel you to beat a dog with a baseball bat. Nenny feels cracked in half.

Still. Cosby is a filthy, filthy animal. In another place, in another time, in some other world, Nenny buries her face in Cosby's fur and reveals all her secrets and sorrows, all the things she's dying to have someone hear.

In this life, though, it is just too much: that filth and mange are just too, too much. Nenny will pet her, sure, but only while wearing gloves. She simply can't imagine touching that fur with her bare hands.

Windsor

THERE'S SOMETHING about Charles and Kat's mom that isn't like anyone Nenny knows—or kinda knows. Nenny's only met her a few times. Her name is Windsor and she wears beautiful clothes, like cowboy boots and ankle-length skirts and a necklace with a white crystal on a long silver chain. Her hands are covered in turquoise rings the size of small plates, and she wears a tasseled leather coat and five or six bracelets on each arm. She looks like the kind of lady you'd see in a movie, smoking at a pay phone outside some bar—but she isn't. She drives a beat-up car, a car that looks scooped from the trash, but you can tell she doesn't care. She lives in Apple Valley, which is over an hour away.

Windsor comes to drop off Charles and Kat, and stands in the living room brushing her hair from her eyes. Her earrings are hoops, her smile wide and toothy like Kat's, her teeth big and crooked like Kat's, freckles like distant stars speckled across her cheeks.

"How about some tea?" Mom offers, like *Stay awhile, have a seat,* but Windsor flips a hand toward the door.

"Oh no, I should get going," she says. When Windsor comes,

she always brings little gifts, small things like gumballs or those free mints you get at restaurants, and she brings one for each of them, because she's the kind of woman who thinks of them all. She chitchats with Mom and Rick about the weather, about her job driving a delivery van, and smiles toothy and bright, bearing little gifts and looking something like a lyric from a song.

It's no secret that her new husband is a lousy drunk. He gets tanked and pushes her around in front of the kids.

"You sure?" Mom says. "I've already got a kettle going."

"No, it's okay. I should get going. It's such a long drive." An hour drive along mountain roads and down desert highways, home to a husband named Gabe, who prefers whiskey sours but will settle for Bud Light, who drives a Ford pickup and last month put his fist through a wall. Really, she must be getting on, it's so dark already, it's such a long drive. Windsor comes in her crappy car, hugs Mom and Rick and high-fives Nenny and the boys, wraps her arms around Kat and Charles like she can't stand to leave them, like each day in their absence is a small torture impossible to bear.

But Windsor doesn't go, not right away. Kat goes upstairs to call her boyfriend and Charles stands by his mother, uncharacteristically quiet. Windsor's bracelets clang like a three-ring circus as she brushes at her hair, and she'll pass on the tea because she really must go, she really should be getting on, and still, but still, she doesn't go.

20/20

MASKED MEN have no scruples. They'll just walk right into your house like they own the place, start pushing you around and manhandling all your things. "Is this real china?" they'll say before knocking whole shelves of plates to the floor. They're ruthless and clumsy and hungry for anything of value, even if it's just your sense of security—which they cannot sell but which makes them feel rich.

This is going to happen to the house on Kensington Drive—raw, uncut, in-your-face home invasion—because it's all the suburban rage. Gangs of black-clad men, bearing knives and sawed-off shotguns and hardly older than teens, could come bursting through the door at any minute and violate you and your family and everything you stand for and hold dear. Which is why the door must be locked, morning, noon, and night. Period.

Strangely, this revelation about masked men does not come from Mom—who won't even keep rubber bands in the house because she treated a kid once who'd had one shot in his eye—but from Rick, who saw it on *20/20*. Home invasions have sprung up around the country like a rash. He makes an announcement at dinner one night, like it's common knowledge and common sense.

"I want you guys to start locking the doors when you come in. They need to stay locked."

Kat looks like he's offended every fiber of her being. Simple requests can do that to her. *"Why?"* she snarls, her lip curled, her eyes ablaze.

"Because I said so, that's why." Rick can get a sort of half growl going when he wants to, like a cat that does not want to be held.

A moment passes while they eat. It's soup and crackers night because Mom's at work, and everyone hates soup and crackers night, so they're all a little on edge.

"Yeah, but why?" Charles finally asks, and because he annoys Rick less than Kat, Rick lays down his spoon and begins to explain.

"Well, I don't want to alarm anyone," he says, which isn't exactly what to say when you're trying not to alarm anyone, "but I saw a report on the news about home invasions. It's probably not going to happen, but we can never be too careful."

There's no way he'd say any of this if Mom were home. Tiny and Nenny look at each other, eyes bugged. This is not the kind of thing they want to hear, not ever, and especially not when Mom's gone.

"What's a home invasion?" Charles asks. There's not the least bit of worry on his face, because Charles isn't fazed by anything and, also, he's kind of weird.

"Well, son. It's when strangers with masks and guns come into your house and try to rob you."

Clearly, this is the wrong thing to say.

"What?" Kat yells, and Nenny feels like she might cry. And why shouldn't she? Bands of armed men storming into the house? What the hell? Even Bubbles looks terrified. He's not the most imaginative, but it doesn't take a rocket scientist to connect the dots between masked men and certain threat.

"I mean, what I mean is..." Rick starts to backtrack immediately, but it's hard to recover from an announcement like this. "Think about it. What with this economic downturn. People are just trying to make ends meet. It's just...they're... desperate. They've got bills too, you know!" All the stupid spilling out of his mouth overcomes him, and now he's just sputtering words. If there's one thing Rick hates, it's stupid words spilling out of mouths. "It's not a big deal. Just keep the damn doors locked!"

Everyone stares at their soup. Nenny wishes desperately that Mom was here. Things always feel easier when Mom is here.

Suddenly, Rick gets up and throws his bowl in the sink. Which is strange too because Rick is crazy about dishes piled in the sink. Without a word, he stomps upstairs.

"Freaky," Charles finally says, and who knows if he's talking about masked men or Rick. After a while someone gets up and begins clearing the table, and then everyone else starts to clean up too. No one says much of anything until Mom gets home.

They're watching TV when she does. When Nenny hears the door open, she nearly jumps out of her skin — *This is it! Masked men!* — but then Mom comes in and there's an audible sigh from everyone.

"Why all the glum faces?" she asks, putting down her purse.

"We thought you was a masked man," Tiny says, taking his thumb from his mouth.

"A what?" So Tiny explains. Something twitches in Mom's

eye, and she doesn't even say anything, just nods and excuses herself upstairs.

Next thing you know, arguing through the big bedroom door. It's hard to hear much, even though the TV's down, except Mom screaming, "They're just kids!" and then more muffled arguing, and then more, until finally the whole thing ends when Rick shouts, "Just make sure they lock the fucking doors!"

FEAR #7: HOME INVASION

MASKED MEN have no scruples. They'll just come right into your house like they own the place, start pushing you around and grabbing all your things. "What's this? Is this a Nintendo? Are these *real* Nike shoes?" They'll knock stuff around and threaten to kick the dog. ("Hey! Don't do that! That's our dog!") They're mean and they're jerk-faced and they don't care about anyone but themselves—which is how come Kat and them are going to get along.

It's likely going to occur when Mom and Rick go out one day, leaving Kat in charge. This always happens. They go off to do something fun, like buy groceries at Costco or bring food to Gramma B, and Nenny and the boys are stuck with Kat, who could make a total snoozefest out of the most glittering parade. She makes them lunch but has no concern for what they like, so it ends up being stacks of mayonnaise and tomato sandwiches, gross pickly things, the kind of crap only she would consume. She lets them watch TV but only what she wants to watch, and once she even has a boy over—which is so against the rules it could melt your face.

Anyway, that's what's happening when the men break in: nothing. Life with Kat is a terrible bore.

"Mayonnaise sandwiches, *again?* I hate mayonnaise!" Charles says.

"Yeah! Mayonnaise is poop!" Tiny pipes in.

"Eat your lunch or no TV," Kat warns.

"Who cares? We only watch what you want to anyway—"

Suddenly there's a rattling at the door.

"Hey, did you guys lock the—" Bubbles starts but doesn't finish, because just then *bam!* Three masked men come bursting in!

"Shut up! All of you! Everyone on the floor!"

Bubbles and Nenny dive to the floor because they always do what they're told. (It's one thing to sass a nun; it's another to sass a masked man.) Tiny doesn't move, just sobs. Charles, on the other hand, leaps onto his chair like there's going to be a show, and Kat stands near the table with a hand on her hip, like *What the hell do you want?*

Are all of Nenny's fears this elaborate? Pretty much.

"I *said*, everyone on the floor." The masked man steps toward Kat, making as though he's going to knock her out or something, and she goes, "Uh, fi-ine," like it's two words, and lies down.

"You too, champ," he says to Charles, who happily jumps to the carpet. A bad guy called him *champ!* He's beaming.

There are three of them: a short one, a tall one, and one Nenny can tell is a lady because she has enormous breasts. The short one's doing all the yelling, so clearly he's in charge.

"All right. Show us where you keep the dough," he growls.

"Dough? What do you want dough for?" Bubbles asks.

Charles rolls his eyes. "He means cash, dummy."

"There is no cash, so just scram," Bubbles, suddenly brave, says from the floor. That's Bubbles for you: full of surprises.

"Bullshit," the little one says. He reeks of cologne and cheap hair gel. "We know your dad's got a secret stash."

"He's not our dad," Tiny says.

"He's my dad," Charles says.

"Yeah, and mine," Kat says.

"Shut up," Bubbles says, glancing at the masked men.

"You shut up," Charles says.

"Screw you."

"Screw *you!*"

Suddenly Charles and Bubbles are up off the floor, lunging for each other's throats, which is strange because Bubbles never fights back.

"Okay, all right." The lady steps in. She pushes the boys away from each other and stands between them, a hand on each of their chests. Charles and Bubbles are seething, they're just about to tear each other up, rip each other limb from limb, when all of a sudden they realize, simultaneously, like they've been struck by some mysterious spell, that the woman has ginormous breasts. Their eyes glaze over and fixate right on her boobs. It's like watching someone get hypnotized on TV.

"Everybody, shut up!" the little one yells, even though no one's said anything for like a minute. Tiny and Nenny are curled together under the table, crying, their arms entwined. The interesting thing about an annoying little brother is that when masked men burst into your house, he's not all that annoying anymore. It's nice for Nenny to have someone to cling to.

"Go upstairs and find the dough," the little one barks, and the tall one scrambles off like an obedient dog. How'd the little one get to be in charge? What kind of life is that, where you just throw on a mask and everyone's at your command?

"Tie 'em up," he says to the lady, but he doesn't even look at her boobs—he looks right at her face, right into her eyes. It occurs to Nenny that they're probably in love.

Charles offers to help tie everyone up, then gleefully receives his own bit of rope. They all listen to the tall one rummaging upstairs: drawers banging open and closed, lots of clomping around. The stupid dog doesn't even bark or try to save them. You can hear her in the other room, snoring by the TV.

Tiny starts telling one of his dumb stories. "Manny Hernandez, his dad's a security guard at a bank, an' one time a robber came in and said, 'Put all the money in this bag!' an' Manny's dad, he was brave, an' he hit that robber right in the head and knockded him out cold."

"Does that kid ever shut up?" the little one asks. He shouts, "Hey, kid! How about you shut up?"

"Yeah, Tiny," Charles says. "Shut up." So Tiny does.

After a minute or so of quiet, the little one says, "So...your parents leave you guys alone often?"

"No. Yes. No," Kat says, but she's just not that into it, constructing a convincing lie.

The lady starts eating one of the sandwiches, her red lips showing through the hole in her mask. "These are pretty good. Did you make these?"

"Yeah," Kat says, perking up.

"Is that mayonnaise? I love mayonnaise," and the little guy starts munching one too.

"Why are you guys doing this?" Kat asks, not mad, just curious. They love her sandwiches, so now they're all best friends. Kat and the masked people are gonna run off to some mall somewhere, steal loads of Guess jeans, gorge themselves on those nasty mall pretzels with the melty cheese.

The little one, whose default is clearly defensive anger, barks, "Because we want to!" He looks down at them on the floor and must realize this isn't a court of law, because then he softens.

"Well, you know, also times are tough. What with this economic downturn. We're just trying to make ends meet."

"We've got bills too, you know," the lady adds.

Kat nods sagely, like *Ah yes, bills, of course.*

The tall one comes back. The other two rush to meet him, but the bizarre thing is, he's not carrying much. Isn't he supposed to have a giant pillowcase stuffed to the brim? Candlesticks and whatnot? Instead, he appears to be cradling something in his hands.

"Boss! You'll never believe what I found," he says, and the other two rush to him.

"Oh my!" the woman says.

"Yes! Yes!" the little one cries. This is it! They've found it! They've finally found the thing that will set them free!

But what is it? The kids are all wriggling around on the floor, straining their necks to see. After an eternity, the woman steps aside so they can get a glimpse. Nenny gasps.

If Nenny expected some kind of massive diamond, even in her imagination, that's not what she sees. It isn't jewelry; it isn't Rick's secret pile of cash. It's not a gold brick, nor is it some priceless antique. Rather, it's a little stuffed dinosaur, no bigger than the tall one's hand: bright purple, with warm stitched-on eyes and shiny plush scales. Dad bought it for Nenny on a whim—he saw it at the mall and thought she might like it, and he was right: she loves it.

It's the most valuable thing in the world.

"Well done," the little one crows and claps the tall one on the back. The masked people start cackling at their big find, even the lady, who for a minute there actually seemed kind of nice. Nenny feels like she's been kicked in the gut.

And then, like that, they're gone. They don't even bother untying the ropes.

DIY

Cosby gets a boil on her neck so Mom and Rick decide to pop it outside. The dog looks uncomfortable and displeased. They lay an old towel out on the patio concrete and, on another, smaller towel, a neat arc of surgical supplies: a scalpel; some masks and gloves; alcohol and little cotton pads; some old rags to stop any bleeding that might occur; a second scalpel in case the first is dull, which it probably is. There's also a brand-new syringe, sweating in its plastic sleeve, and a bottle of lidocaine that Rick stole from the hospital supply room—which is, of course, totally illegal. This is a true story.

They've been fighting about it all afternoon.

"On the patio? For Chrissake, Rick!" Mom never says "for Chrissake," so this is the real deal. She's pissed.

"This is nursing school stuff, Marie. Level one."

"It's barbaric!"

"It'll take fifteen minutes and then we'll be done. I promise."

"Why can't we just take her to a vet, for Chrissake?"

But Mom already knows the answer to that, so it's silly to even ask. They can't take Cosby to the vet because Cosby is a gas station dog, not some kind of purebred wonder, and you just don't take gas station dogs to the vet. Of course Rick would never say this out loud, and who knows if he's even aware that he thinks it, but from all the evidence—the discount dog food, the fact that she doesn't own any toys, no one takes her for walks (come to think of it, does she even have a leash?), she sleeps on a mat in the garage, and there's a boil on her neck that they've let grow to the size of a grapefruit—the thinking is clear: a gas station dog is just not worth it.

The kids aren't allowed to watch, but they do anyway. Mom and Rick's window is on the second floor and looks straight down onto the patio, and since the patio is an ongoing work in progress (another fight), it lacks a roof. It's like sitting in the mezzanine above a surgical floor. They press their foreheads against the glass.

"We should open the window," Bubbles says.

"What for?" Nenny asks.

"So we can see better."

"Yeah! And smell the blood!" Charles says.

Tiny wrinkles his nose. "That's gwoss."

"Shut up!" Kat finally says. "We're not going to open the window because they'll know we're here." She's such a snot, but she makes a good point. Sometimes the flailing body needs a head, and painful as it is to admit, Kat is the head.

They fall silent and their breath fogs up the window. The surgery hasn't started quite yet. There's all these elaborate pre-surgery rituals Mom's going through, lots of petting and cooing. Rick's busy sharpening blades and loading up the syringe. The whole thing is kind of awful—one story up, and Nenny can sense Mom's horror and sorrow. How had they let it get this far? What have they become? And Nenny can see (God, how she can see) that if Mom could magically zip back through time to that moment at the gas station when a scraggly old mutt jumped into the car, she would, she'd go right back: take the dog to a vet and a grooming salon, get her washed up real nice, claws clipped, fur trimmed. Mom would go back to every morning they've had her and take the dog for a walk, for Chrissake, and give her a name that *meant something*—not just some stupid thing that happened to be on TV.

But there's no such thing as zipping back through time. She leans in close and puts her nose against the dog's nose and nuzzles behind its ears. Rick's ready. He flicks the syringe like they do on TV and then it's in and Cosby goes floppy and relaxed and lies very still. Rick opens his fingers, and Mom lays the scalpel in his hand.

What happens next is kind of expected and not really a big deal: Rick makes the first cut. The blade doesn't glint in the sunlight; blood doesn't come squirting out. Rick just makes a small incision and there's a little bit of blood but not much, and Mom hands him some gauze to press on the wound. It's all very measured and slow.

"Is that it?" Charles says, because he's a boy and boys always want more blood.

"Quiet!" Kat snaps and again puts her face against the glass.

Then something does happen, and it's subtle and awful at once. Rick's removed the gauze, the scalpel's in his hand, he's ready for the next cut, but then this thing happens, this tiny little thing, and if you weren't paying rapt attention with your face against the glass you'd hardly notice it at all: a tiny flicker of hesitation stills his hand. It's one of those things you're not even sure you saw but you *know* you saw it, and the way it feels is like a minute ripple wriggling across the surface of the universe. It has meaning because Rick was in Vietnam, and though Nenny doesn't know much about Vietnam, she knows this: you don't hesitate if you were in Vietnam. Men who hesitate didn't come home from Vietnam, because the men who hesitated are dead.

Mom looks at him then because she felt it too, that naked trace of doubt, but Rick doesn't even look at her, and he moves on because the moment has passed.

Then, there's blood. Lots and lots of blood. Even from a story up, you can see it gushing, pouring onto the concrete, matting up Cosby's fur. Mom frantically starts scooping up gauze, and then more gauze, then more. The bleeding doesn't stop, and the dog starts twitching and whimpering, clearly confused, and Mom is panicking and then Rick's panicking too, and he's scrambling to tip Cosby up, to somehow contain the flow, and Charles yells, "Oh shit!" and covers his mouth with his hand, and there's blood all over the patio, there's blood all over Mom and Rick, and all those walks that no one's taking start adding up to miles, miles and miles and miles, because suddenly that gas station mutt has become the family dog.

Kat loses it then. Tiny is crying and Bubbles is nervously flapping his hands and Charles is cursing up a storm and Nenny doesn't know what to feel because she's feeling everything at once—and Kat just loses her shit.

"What the fuck is going on!" She slaps her hand against the glass. Mom and Rick look up, and it's clear they had no idea the kids were there. Mom reaches up and pulls the mask off her face, and if the kids expect disappointment or anger, that's not the look they get. They get another look altogether, which is a mix of fear and profound regret. It's a look for when they've all seen something they should not have seen.

Kat's still shouting and then she's throwing open the door.

They hear her booming down the stairs, and then the outside door bangs open, and now they're looking down at the top of her head too.

"This is so fucked! It's totally inhumane!" It's the first time she's said a word bigger than herself, so this is serious. She snatches up the surgical towel and the implements go crashing across the concrete. She kneels and presses the towel into Cosby's neck, who's still whimpering and shaking a little like a trembling leaf. This goes on for a long time: Kat holding that towel in place, Mom's hand on her back. Even all the way from a story up, you can tell they're crying. Rick sits beside them and stares.

And then that's it. It's not really a big deal anymore. Turns out Rick hit an arterial vein, whatever that means. He manages to bundle Cosby up and get her to a vet, who puts stitches in her neck and fixes the wound. After that she's fine, even though for a while she has bandages wrapped all around her neck and head that require changing. There might be a small shift, because the universe had rippled and all—a couple of occasional walks, someone buys a chew toy, Kat lets the dog sleep on her bed. But then Kat gets a new boyfriend and isn't around much anymore, and everyone else mentions a walk here and there, but then they forget. Nenny still pets the dog, every now and then. Sometimes, she doesn't. Sometimes, it's just too much work to go and fetch the gloves.

King of the Rats

WHAT CHARLES does at night is anyone's guess. It is October and the streets are filled with leaves.

Late, when it is safe to do so, when everyone else has gone to bed and the house hums with sleep, Charles closes the door to his and Bubbles's room and ties two sets of sheets together, end to end to end. The trick lies in treating the corners before you tie, taking the cloth between your thumb and forefinger and rolling back and forth, back and forth, until each sheet comes to a perfect point. Bubbles, who is afraid of everything, who gets squeamish around lizards and snakes, who balks at things other boys delight in—mud and worms and war and the rusted-metal taste of their own blood—huddles in his bed against the wall, his own sheets fist-balled beneath his chin, eyes like a scared rabbit's and a shaking in his voice he cannot control.

"Where are you going?" he whispers, and it's like trying to cut glass with a slipper. Sad, really, the space between the world and some boys.

"Out," Charles says, matter-of-factly, as he slides the window open. He doesn't even glance down, just tosses out the giant ball of sheet. It lands with a quiet thump a story below. He checks the tension of the bed-tied end, once, before climbing up on the ledge. He doesn't say anything before he goes, and he never says anything when he gets back, but every night Bubbles imagines that he does. "G'night," Charles says in the stone silence after he's actually gone. "G'night, Bubbles" or "Be right back." Every night Bubbles imagines it, not because he wants to but because he has to. It's the only way that he can sleep.

— ⁕ —

Nenny will spend a lot of time in the coming years thinking about all of this, the details that cocoon these nights: the moon's light pooling in the midnight streets, Bubbles trembling in his bed, the distant passing of cars. Or she'll imagine Kat, kissing her new boyfriend on the little knoll in the front yard. His name is Jeremy and he's obsessed with kachina dolls because his great-great something or other was an Indian chief. He's gonna get a tattoo about it someday.

"Where's your brother going at night anyway?" he says when they're done, which is probably a weird thing to say after kissing someone. If it wasn't for his warrior lineage and the fact that he's in a band, Kat would have dumped him weeks ago.

"What are you talking about?" That glare of hers that could slice through walls.

But then—or so Nenny imagines—Jeremy points, and Kat is shocked that no one's noticed before: a ragged and obvious bald patch is etched into the ivy beneath the boys' window, as if someone is taking a machete to it every night. Kat is so excited she doesn't mind that Jeremy can't kiss very well, and he's a genius and a warrior all over again.

There's also this: Meli Sampsell was this girl who used to go to Sacred Heart, and she just talked and talked all day. She talked so much that Nenny didn't even care when she moved away. Meli supposedly had this cousin with Barrette's disease. Or...what is it? The one where you twitch all over the place and they have to tie you to your chair so you won't fall on the floor. The cousin was on *60 Minutes* even, and his mom was just like blushing and blushing, because in addition to twitching all over the place he also said "Shitfuckfart! Shitfuckfart!" That was part of the disease too, "Shitfuckfart!" He couldn't help himself. And isn't that sad? Isn't that so sad? (Meli Sampsell, the first in their class to have braces, all that metal glinting in her face.) Anyway, her *other* cousin—the Barrette cousin's brother—he, like, couldn't even stand it anymore. It was "Shitfuckfart!" all day and then his brother lands on TV? Like, he loved his brother and all, but, *God*, can you even imagine? So the brother? He just totally snapped.

And anyone listening to the story—for the first time, anyway—probably had some notion of what snapping looked like, but it wasn't that kind of snapping at all. The brother didn't go on a killing rampage or anything like you'd expect. Instead, he became a sort of steward of the night. (Where did Meli even learn that word?) He got his hands on a bunch of cave-diving gear and made this equipment belt loaded with whatever he'd need: some rope and hooks, a couple of those clippy things that only open one way. He wore one of those extra-strong head-lamps that miners wear when they're inside caves, because that's what he was doing, that's exactly what Barrette's brother was doing every night: sneaking out to explore the city's bowels. His brother had this terrible disease and his mom was dying of confusion and shame, and he just couldn't take it anymore, so he loaded himself down with gear and spent his time mapping the sewers at night. Supposedly they found all the maps later, his dad like "Son, what *is* this?" and his mom just crying some more. Of course there was never any real evidence that he played with rats, but that's what Meli called him anyway and that's the part that stuck: King of the Rats. He had them trained: he'd give one long sharp whistle and they'd all come running, from every corner of the city, eager and prepared to do his bidding.

"He had them trained?" someone was bound to ask, because of course it sounded totally fake, like the plot to some stupid cartoon.

"*Trained,*" Meli'd say, with such conviction that it became the truth.

Anyway, that's what Nenny thinks of when Kat breaks the news—the King of the Rats. Kat comes in and throws her purse onto the bed and proclaims, "Charles is in so much shit!" Her eyes are like two polished stones. But when Kat tells her the big news, Nenny can't picture the gnawed-up ivy or the two-story drop to the ground. All she sees is a sea of rodents and Charles, arms raised, floating on their backs.

Kat's out like a light within minutes, but Nenny can't sleep. She listens for the sound of something but she does not know what. Is this what it sounds like? What does it sound like? Feet crashing through ivy? Sneakers on pavement? Can he hear all the blood pulsing in his lungs? Do dogs bark when he runs by? Or some guy, someone's dad or something, "Hey, what's that kid doing out there?" What sound does a sewage grate make? What's moonlight sound like when you're climbing down a hole? She can picture the *drip, drip, dripping,* because they play that sound on *Ninja Turtles* all the time, but what's the sound of one rat scratching? Twenty rats? A thousand? What's the sound of a narrow tunnel when you're the only light? And can he hear anything from above anymore? Does he hear cars passing overhead? If he stands directly beneath the house, what then? What's the sound of a whole house sleeping? Or mostly sleeping but a little wide-awake? If your stepsister cannot sleep, does she make a sound? And if she does, is it audible? Can you even hear it over the din of all those rats?

Spoiled

ONE SATURDAY the washing machine breaks and the dryer's close behind, and Mom says, "God dammit!" and slams the lid.

"Nenny, go find some quarters."

"Quarters? Why quarters?" A hope bright and brief as a Skee-Ball scoreboard flashes through her.

"*Because*. Why do you think?" Mom's words are clipped and angry. She starts half slamming, half stacking things by the door—a box of detergent, baskets overflowing with clothes—while Nenny goes from room to room, hunting for quarters. It's like trying to find rice in a hill of sand. She finds two in the drawer by the phone, a third in the paper-clip cup, and one under the couch. Not very promising.

"Give me some quarters," she says to Charles, who's on the dungeon level of Mario even though he's already beat it a million times.

"What in the hell for?" he asks, but she sets her jaw and bugs her eyes in a way that says *It's Mom, you dweeb*, and he catches the drift and runs upstairs. He comes back with a half-full sock—the only clean sock in the house, probably—and thrusts it at Nenny.

"She'd better pay me back."

Even though Mom's pissed, she lets Nenny come along and softens halfway through the drive. She's like that: prone to rage and then gentle guilt for exposing the kids to her wrath.

"You ever been to a laundromat before?" she asks.

"I don't think so," Nenny says. It feels somehow unjust. Isn't laundry, like, a great American pastime? Dad's apartment building has a laundry room, but it hardly counts because it's in the basement and only has two machines. "I guess not."

Mom smiles. "Boy, are you spoiled!" She looks at Nenny playfully, but Nenny just looks back. She sure doesn't feel spoiled. Spoiled is a new Barbie every week and trips to the skating rink. Spoiled's not sharing a room with Kat, who honks when she snores.

"What I mean is, some families don't have their own machines. Some families have to use the laundromat."

Have to? More like get to. Spudz Sudz is as wonderful as it sounds. A smiling cartoon potato scrubs itself on the front window, bubbles floating up to spell out the name. The unclear connection between a potato and laundry seems beside the point. For a dollar fifty a load, you can wash *and* dry your clothes while taking full advantage of the magazine rack (free) and, best of all, the bank of candy dispensers by the door (two quarters for a handful, worth every cent).

Mom and Nenny practically have the place to themselves, which feels lucky. Mom lets Nenny pick out their machine, then dumps the clothes in and sprinkles in some Tide. Doing laundry at a laundromat lends the chore a kind of magic. The sound of quarters plunking in! There's plastic chairs for while you wait! The machines sound like a hive of bees!

You want to know what spoiled is? Spoiled is when your mom

takes you, and only you, to a special place like a laundromat and presses two quarters for candy into your hand without being asked.

An old man is sitting next to the candy machines. He's got a newspaper folded in his lap and no laundry or quarters that Nenny can see.

"You getting a gumball?" he asks. There's something about him that Nenny cannot name: his plastic sandals, his hands crooked and bent like gross crabs. Nenny nods.

"Little girls love gumballs, don't they?" He seems to know a lot of little girls.

"Nenny," Mom says, like she's done something wrong.

"Aw, Christ," he says suddenly, smacking his paper on his lap. "I'm just doin' my laundry!"

"We're all just doing our laundry," Mom says and calls Nenny back with her hand.

A woman comes through the door then, and when she sees the old man, she starts yelling something in a language Nenny doesn't understand.

"Aw, Christ!" he shouts again and throws his paper down. "I live in this neighborhood too, you know!" Then, without warning, he slams past the woman and out the door.

"No good," the woman says, shaking her finger at Nenny and Mom. "No good," she says again.

"Yes, no good," Mom says and pulls Nenny close. Nenny has no idea what just happened but suspects it has something to do with the old man's hands, his watery-looking eyes. The woman goes into a room marked EMPLOYEES ONLY and closes the door.

—∿—

Twenty minutes later the laundry's almost done, but Mom says, "Whoo! I've got to pee!" in a way that shows she's been holding it awhile. She takes Nenny's hand and they go to the back of the laundromat. Mom pushes the bathroom door open with her fingertips, then mutters, "Jesus fuck." What's more surprising? That Mom just said those terrible words or what they see: someone has taken a turd and, using it as a kind of pen, smeared shit all over the toilet and sink and walls.

—⁂—

In the car, Mom says, "Here," and thrusts a bottle of hand sanitizer into Nenny's hand. They swipe at their fingers in silence and then drive home, and they never go to a laundromat again.

Chester

MOM AND RICK are going out to dinner so they ask Chester to babysit. Chester's their cousin since Mom married Rick. He's tiny and scrappy and all of eighteen, with a moustache so scraggly it shouldn't be there at all, really, and a kind of dumb sweetness about him like someone spilt bubble gum down his shirt.

"You guys wanna make pizza?" It's just Nenny and the boys because Kat's on a date. They watch Chester with bewildered awe. Eighteen! He can buy cigarettes and dirty magazines if he wants to. He can vote, whatever that means. He can *move out of Uncle Max's house,* for criminy's sake, though he still lives at home, in a room decorated with tiger posters and a faux sheepskin covering half the floor.

Chester pokes through the refrigerator until he finds what he needs. Gingerly, with the quiet skill of a surgeon, he lays four large tortillas across the counter. He coaxes ketchup from a bottle and smears it across them, sweeping his wrist back and forth. Then he piles on layer after layer of Kraft cheese, their plastic skins spilling off the counter to the floor. Four minutes in the microwave and—

"Voilà!" he announces, presenting each of them with a plate. The pizzas look like nuclear fallout victims from TV. Nobody does anything, not even Tiny, who will touch dog poop if you pay him. Nobody except Bubbles, that is, who wolfs down every bite.

Later, Chester says, "Is that a He-Man castle?!" and looks like he's just won a prize. He makes Skeletor and He-Man wrestle to the death. Man-At-Arms scrambles to the top of the castle and does a twisty kind of dance. "Hey, Nenny, you got any Barbies?" He-Man kisses Barbie up against the castle wall, and the way he does it, it's questionable whether Chester's kissed anything before. Barbie shoots through the trapdoor, naked, then puts on a pair of mismatched shoes while Battle Cat chews on an eraser that came from who knows where. Skeletor and Stinkor have an oafish conversation about death.

"You wanna die?"

"*You* wanna die?"

And then Chester can see that everyone's bored, so they all go watch TV. Later, Tiny falls out of his bunk bed—just rolls right out—and lies there crying on the floor. To console him, Chester makes a pot of hot cocoa, but the pot somehow melts all over the stove. The whole house reeks of metal and burnt plastic. Tiny's still lying on the floor.

But Chester? Chester's a pro. They don't pay him $2.50 an hour for nothing, so what does Chester do? He buries the pot in the yard.

Keeping Track

AT THE end of October a new quiet descends upon the house like nothing Nenny's heard before. Though she doesn't know it yet, it's the silent assault of approaching death. Gramma B's been declining for months. That's what they say, "a steady decline," as though she's slowly crawling down a hill. All her things keep showing up. New boxes arrive every day, junk and knickknacks and trinkets caked with dust. Mom says, "Gramma B is cleaning house. She doesn't need all this stuff anymore." But Nenny knows what Mom really means: Gramma B is going to die.

The silence of Rick downstairs in the middle of the night, pretending to read. The silence of every minute when the phone's not ringing, and the nervous anxiety when it does. There's also an unspoken pact among the kids not to fight anymore—not for a while, at least. Let things happen first. Let the silence, you know, pass.

At first there are just seven boxes. Only one of them has a label—"Kitchen"—which is strange because there's not a plate or fork to be seen. "Kitchen" is mostly old T-shirts wrapped around stuff that doesn't really need wrapping: two issues of

Country-Wide magazine, a bundle of plastic bracelets, a stuffed elephant missing an ear. The second box at first seems to be just a tangle of yarn, but at the bottom Nenny finds a bleached white jawbone, probably from a cow. It's Saturday and she's not supposed to be digging through all this stuff. But Mom and Rick are at the hospital, and anyway, who else is gonna keep track of Gramma B's things? The bone weighs as much as a book and still has some teeth attached, and see? Someone's got to take note.

Box three is all Louis L'Amour novels, which is, like, big deal, who cares, but the interesting thing is how Gramma B spent time meticulously underlining in each one: "the sun set fast in the west," "he had a smoky, hardened face," "the old mare knew the way to go." Box four is a silver arm bracelet shaped like a snake, six candles that have never been lit, a denture container with nothing inside, and some tennis balls that clearly belong to Nuisance, that ratty old dog.

Nenny starts to make a pile. Obviously the snake bracelet, and also the tennis balls. She picks up and considers the bone, and—this happens sometimes—the room starts to feel like it has eyes. Not human eyes, but still, so Nenny puts it back. She covers it up with yarn and waits for the tingling in her spine to pass. It always does.

Box five is Christmas decorations, and they're not even the nice kind—just those ugly bulbs that look like hair balls and strings of old lights. Box six holds what looks like a tablecloth but turns out to be a dress. It's printed with swirls and orange leaves, and only takes up a small corner of the box, which is a total waste of space as far as Nenny is concerned. Box seven is all those stinking doilies and a bunch of office supplies. There's not a single animal figurine to be found.

Nenny sighs and lies down on the floor. She bends her knees and puts her feet up against box one, then slowly pushes it as far away from her as it will go. She does the same with box two, scoots her body a little to reach box three, and so on, foot-pushing all the boxes away across the floor. She lies in the middle like a sun at the center of some junk-store universe. She reaches for the snake bracelet and holds it close to her face.

It's weird to call someone "Gramma" who's not, actually, your grandma. One of her grandmas lives in Arizona, and the other died when Nenny was five. She got sick and peed and peed until she couldn't pee anymore and then she died. She was a mean grandma with a secret pocket of nice—like she'd throw out your favorite hat but then give you a bushel of dollar bills for your birthday. If you asked her what was for dinner, she'd say, "Sauerkraut and pigtails," but not in a funny way, in a cranky way. Her first baby had died, curled up against her leg—he would have been Nenny's oldest uncle if he hadn't died—so that probably explained why she was so grumpy all the time.

But Nenny doesn't know anything about Gramma B. Like, what happened to her husband? Or why does she smoke so dang much? What's gonna happen to Nuisance when she dies? No way can he come live here. One stinky old mutt is enough.

Nenny rolls to her side and considers calling Boots—to tell her about the snake bracelet, ask her if she wants a dog—but then remembers that Boots is in Arkansas, visiting *her* grandma. Ugh. She thinks of Frog and Toad. "The whole world is covered in grandmas and none of them are mine!" The house ticks with quiet, because Kat's gone and the boys are all outside.

She stands and lets the snake bracelet tumble into a box. It doesn't even fit anyways. She scoops up the pile of tennis balls—they're crunchy from dried-up old spit—and goes into the TV room, where Cosby's sleeping on the floor. Nenny kneels and places the balls before Cosby's snout—"Here you go, old girl"—but the stupid dog doesn't do anything, doesn't even wake up, just snores.

Ask a Priest

Ask a Priest Day happens once a month and sounds like what it is: one of Sacred Heart's priests goes from class to class, answering questions the students have written on index cards. It's an event at once as exciting and mundane as it sounds. The students are given free rein to ask a priest anything they want, under the protection of absolute anonymity. Which you'd *think* would lend the whole operation a kind of edge—but the truth is that the children of Sacred Heart are a timid, unimaginative bunch. Their questions are pretty lame.

Today Ask a Priest is Father Bill. Sacred Heart has three priests: the nice one, the drunk one, and the one with crusty eyes. Father Chauncey is the drunk one. His face is mottled and red and he smells like the bottom of the Communion cup. The nuns look disgusted whenever he's around. Father Michael is the one with crusty eyes. He looks at you in a way you don't want anyone to look at you, especially not a priest. Then there's Father Bill, the nice one. He knows everyone's name and smiles with Santa Claus wrinkles around his eyes. He never gets grumpy, and he has patience in limitless stores.

"All right," he says, standing at the front of the room. "What will we ask today?" He pulls the first card off the top of the stack. "What is the best way to get into heaven?"

Clearly this is a throwaway question—someone too lazy to come up with a real one—but Father Bill treats each question equally, with the loving calm of a shepherd leading stupid, wayward sheep. "First, love God with all your heart. Turn away from sin and love your neighbor. Say your prayers and do good things." It's nice, though a tad confusing, how simple it all sounds, like a recipe for boiled eggs.

Second question: "Is it wrong to hate my brother? He makes me so mad!"

Answer: "Siblings are sometimes difficult, aren't they?" Father Bill chuckles, and see? That's the thing. Father Chauncey would've just launched into some boring slurred diatribe, but Father Bill gets it. "I have a brother myself. We fought an awful lot when we were boys. He was bigger than me and liked to prove it." Everyone is extra attentive. What a marvelous, bizarre thing—a priest as a boy! "But then our father died"— priests have dads?—"and our mother was very sick"—and moms?—"and my brother and I had to work together and learn to love each other." He pauses and seems to look directly at all of them at once. "Pray that you may love your siblings, and forgive their faults."

For a brief, shimmering moment this seems possible. Now, *that's* a good priest!

Next question: "What do priests eat?"

"Mostly dirt and worms. We're very humble." Boy, that gets a laugh! Even Sister Timothy guffaws and slaps her knee. "But seriously, we eat humbly, and we pray before every meal."

See? The guy's masterful.

Q: "How did you know you wanted to be a priest?"

A: "I didn't know right away. I prayed and prayed for many years until God answered and told me it was the right thing to do. But it's not for everyone." He looks at Sister Timothy, who nods. "It's a life of privation, but it has its rewards."

Nenny pictures wearing nothing but drab-colored clothes and eating food out of label-less cans.

Q: "Why do we have to go to confession if God already knows our sins?"

A: "Think of confession as an apology. God is like us—when He's hurt, He wants us to apologize, and when we sin we hurt God. Confessing is a way of apologizing and restoring our relationship with God."

Q: "Is it a sin to say bad words but only in your head?"

A: "Yes. The Lord knows our thoughts and our hearts. Keep your mind clean and your heart pure."

Ask a Priest lasts for only half an hour, and apparently Nenny's question—Do you ever dream about God?—is not going to be answered, because just then Father Bill shakes a card in the air, smiles, and says, "Okay, last one."

Q: "My father says the Russians want to kill us. Is he right?"

Father Bill's face darkens like a cloud.

A: "The Russians?" Spit from his mouth like a distasteful word. "We should pray for their very souls."

FEAR #22: THE RUSSIANS

SACRED HEART Catholic School is the site of the first American-soil battle of the Cold War. Of course no one knows this, so when the bell sounds a series of rapid-fire alarms, everyone's surprised. "Get under your desks!" Sister Timothy shouts and peers through the blinds. "Oh no, it's the Russians! Dear God, dear God, dear God!" She crosses herself like crossing's the only thing left.

The sound of heavy boots fills the halls. The children cower and tremble beneath their desks. Nenny's knees shake and sweat beads on her lip and she thinks about all the things she'll never do: ride a horse through fields of shimmering grass, become a world-famous rock star/fashion designer, grow boobs. A boot kicks furiously at the door, and the door comes unhinged and flies across the room in a neat arc and lands, *thump*, crushing Sister Timothy at her desk. Too bad.

Mikhail Gorbachev comes into the room. *The* Mikhail Gorbachev. He's flanked by a herd of fierce-but-dim-looking soldiers. He halts them with a flick of his wrist. The room pulses with nervous fear and the terribly unfortunate death of their teacher. Her feet show under the door like in *The Wizard of Oz*.

"Children! American children!" Gorby calls in a singsong. "Come out from under desk now!"

Nobody moves. Katie Marion furiously whispers the Our Father and Michael Barber weeps in a ball. Matty Souza, two rows over, must be keeping his cool, though, because he rolls his pant cuffs in a particular way. It's hard to describe. You pull the hem of your pant taut and crease it with your finger, then roll twice, as tight as you can. All the girls love him and all the boys want to be him. Nenny glances over and for a moment their eyes meet and maybe this is it? Maybe this is love?

But there's no time for love in the Cold War, because Gorby shouts, "I said now!" and everyone scrambles from beneath their desks. Should they sit down? Keep standing? War is very confusing.

The general secretary of the Communist Party of the Soviet Union stands at the front of their classroom, his birthmark throbbing beneath the fluorescent lights. He's round and stern, and there's snow, for some reason, on his coat. He brushes the snow off with his hand.

"Now everyone sit," he commands. The children all sit, and the soldiers do too, because they're clearly morons.

"Ne ty, idioty!" he yells in Russian, and they scramble to their feet. Gorby casts them a glance that could freeze continents.

"So this is America," he says then, sweeping his hand. "Land of free, home of brave." He spits on the floor. *"Moya noga!"* He stomps, and the children shiver and quake. "The tyranny of America has gone on long enough! We will no longer be America's fool."

If you think this whole thing is strange, it's not. For months Nenny has suspected that the Gorbachev from the news— magnanimous, beloved, waving at crowds or shaking Reagan's hand—is all part of some trick, just another move in a years-long war. Think of a game of night tag: your best friend could turn out to be your fiercest opponent. Never trust smiles and handshakes. Even Nenny knows that, and she's only eight.

Gorby goes to the desk and motions with his hand. The soldiers march over and lift the fallen door. Sister Timothy is flat as a board.

"Remove this vile specimen of church," Gorby commands, and they scoop her up and toss her out the door. Katie Marion crosses herself and begins to cry. Gimme a break.

"Enough!" Gorby shouts in her face. The Russians are hard ice-pick men, and ice-pick men neither pray nor cry. Isn't that what this whole thing is about anyway? The right to pray, cry, wave flags, eat hot dogs and a wide variety of packaged cakes?

"As soon as American girl is done whimpering like weak dog, we play game." Everyone glares at Katie, like *Shut your blubbering hole,* and finally she does.

A game? How exciting! A giant wheel appears and lively music plays. WIN THE WAR shines in dazzling lights. A mechanical arm comes out of nowhere and plops a toupee on Gorby's glowing pate, then hands him a sparkling cape.

"Win! The! War!" the soldiers shout, and everyone cheers. Everyone except Nenny. She's got the ominous feeling this isn't like other games. It resembles Wheel of Fortune but likely has higher stakes.

"Our first contestant, Matty Souza from Somerset Lane!" The crowd goes wild as Matty jogs to the front of the room.

"Matty, tell us about yourself."

"Well, I like to roll my pant cuffs in a particular way. It drives the girls crazy—"

"Enough!" Gorby's face darkens. "Spin wheel."

Matty gives the wheel a weak spin. It lands on TELEVISION AND FILM.

"America's favorite pastime: wasting useless brains," Gorby says, and all the Russians laugh. Matty looks puzzled. "Never mind, American weakling. Answer this." He pulls a stack of note cards from his pocket. "What 1985 film begins realistically enough, when strong, menacing Russian boxer pummels American to death, but ends ridiculously with another American winning in ring?"

Matty appears momentarily baffled, but the synopsis is obvious, though skewed.

"*Rocky Four*?" he says, looking up at Gorby.

Ding! Ding! Ding! Bells sound and the wheel flickers. "You are correct, American scum. Welcome to Red Army." Two soldiers slap a uniform on Matty, and everyone cheers. Now they all want to be in the Red Army. They go, "Ooh! Ooh! Me! Me!" waving their hands, hoping to be picked, except Nenny, who's no fool.

"You, weakling with pale face," Gorby says, calling Steve Smoot from the crowd. Steve's perfect for the Red Army—he hasn't got half a brain. The wheel lands on OUTER SPACE.

"What is name of satellite proud Russians sent to space in order to demonstrate our marked superiority over brainless Americans?"

"Oh, I know this." How in God's name does Steve Smoot know this? "*Sputnik!*"

"That is correct, American scum. Welcome to Red Army." They slap a uniform on Steve, and he gives Matty a high five.

This goes on—who's Edward Lee Howard, define "bolshe-vism," where is Lenin's body and how is it preserved—and everyone gets a uniform and everyone cheers. Finally, there's only Nenny remaining. Admittedly, she's torn: she knows that Communist life is a life of privation, a life of drab-colored clothes and food in label-less cans. Still, she hates to be left out.

"Ah, little girl! What charming American girl." Gorby stoops and pinches her cheek. She winces.

"Little girl, are you ready for Big Question?"

Nenny's not sure, but she nods anyway.

"Are you ready to win war?"

"Yes?"

"Good." His lip curls and he turns to the soldiers. "Bring me red phone."

There's an audible intake of breath as someone produces the phone. Everyone knows about the red phone. The red phone has only one button, and it doesn't dial anywhere but straight to hell. The red phone's never been used, because it can be used only once. A call on the red phone means that's it, *poof*. The end of life as we know it.

"Now spin wheel." The evil in his voice is pronounced. In a few months Mikhail Gorbachev will come to speak at the United Nations and practically declare an end to the Cold War. People will celebrate and cheer. His name will be chanted in the streets. He'll be on the cover of *Time* magazine. Even then, though, Nenny will think: How do you end a war with just one speech? If war could end with just speeches, why aren't people giving more speeches?

Now the phone glows beneath Gorby's hand while the wheel spins and spins. Where will it land, Nenny? Wherever will it land?

Sheila Collins

BACK BEFORE all this—before Mom married Rick at the county courthouse at the far end of the Vegas strip (celebrating with an all-you-can-eat buffet); before Kat and Charles and all their things; before shared bedrooms and milk with dinner and a color-coded chart with weekly chores, wrestling matches in front of the TV, screaming fights over who said what to whom, family trips where everyone is irritable and bored; before all this shuttling back and forth, endlessly, between houses, wearing a path so distinct and persistent and thin you might see it from the moon; before the walls started pushing in and they had to learn to share more and more of less and less space—*way* back, ancient history back, there was a woman named Sheila Collins.

In photos crammed in a forgotten drawer, Sheila Collins is roly-poly round and has a pale and doughy face. She looks as though someone thumb-pressed her eyes. Charles won't talk about her at all, goes completely silent at the mention of her name. And it's no use asking Rick, because he doesn't like kids poking around. Nenny knows that if she asks, she'll just get a lecture about minding her own.

It comes up because Sheila Collins dies. One Saturday morning Mom's reading the paper, and suddenly she makes a sound like *ha-uh*, like being punched, and she claps a hand over her mouth and looks like she might cry.

"What is it?" Nenny asks, though it's no rare thing for Mom to read the paper and cry.

"Sheila Collins died," Mom says, her eyes fixed on the print. The fridge hums, and it's strange how no one is around.

"Who is Sheila, anyways?" Nenny asks. She's heard bits here and there but not enough to fit all the pieces together.

"Oh, Sheila." Mom sighs and shakes her head. "Sheila wasn't well." And leaves it at that, as if that were enough.

Kat is the only one willing to talk, but of course Nenny has to ply her with compliments first. *Your crimp looks really cool and your outfit is amazing, also who's Sheila Collins?* It's a few hours later because Kat's been at the mall. They're standing in the kitchen, and when Nenny says it, a look moves over Kat's face like she's seen a ghost, and maybe she has.

"Why?! Is she here?"

"No, she died. It was in the paper."

The look passes and a new one appears. Kat's teenage mouth goes agape, and Nenny can see all the brackets and silver shining inside.

"She died? Sheila fucking Collins *died?*"

"Yeah. But who is she?"

"How did Sheila Fat-Ass Collins die?"

"I don't know. Di-a-something or other. You eat too much sugar and then your liver explodes. It was in the paper. Who knows."

Suddenly, Kat throws her head back and laughs. "That is so perfect! That is so fucking perfect!" she howls. "That fat whore ate herself to death!"

"Yeah but, Kat...who *is* she?"

Kat leans back then, crosses her arms and puts her hip against the counter. This is the most she's talked to Nenny, ever. She thrusts her neck forward and swings her head so there's a little punch in all her words.

"*Sheila Collins* is a *no*-good, *white trash, nas*ty, dis*gus*ting pig *bitch*." She lets these words sink in before delivering the final blow. "And I'm fucking *glad* she's dead."

Nenny, on her life, has never heard such a stream of vitriol and filth before. Also, it's quite possible there's some sisterly bonding going on.

"What did she *do?*" Even though she's already hanging on Kat's every word, it's important for Nenny to *show* that she's hanging on Kat's every word. She bugs her eyes and lets her arms kind of dangle at her sides, like that cartoon wolf that's always picking his jaw up off the ground. Kat lives to have someone—anyone—hang on her every word.

"I'll tell you, but make me a sandwich first." Oh, she's good. Real good. The sandwich: turkey with lettuce and cheddar and a dash of (swear to God) Marshmallow Fluff. Nenny holds her tongue and delivers the sandwich on a plate. She watches, pained, while Kat makes a big show of eating. They both know this is part of the game, but Nenny plays along. She observes Kat with feigned patience, like pretending to watch a god eat when it's more like feeding time at the zoo. Damn if Kat can't drag things out.

"How 'bout some juice?" she says, so Nenny scrambles to get that too. Kat takes long, slow glugs, breathing through her nose, then leans her head back and lets out a sky-shattering belch. She picks up her napkin and dabs the corners of her mouth in false demure.

Finally, the story begins.

"Dad met Sheila at the hospital, working nights. She was somehow miraculously in charge of the nurses' station—I guess they wanted a fat retard in charge in those days. Who knows. Anyway, for some reason that's impossible to explain, he started dating her. I *doubt* he asked her out—she probably stalked him all over the halls begging him for a date, and he finally said yes because he was desperate and lonely. Mom had already divorced him and had a new boyfriend, so he knew he may as well move on—"

"Wait, she divorced *him?*"

"What do you mean?"

"I don't know, I just thought…" Nenny trailed off. For some reason she thought it was the other way around, not that it matters.

"Do you want to hear the story or not?" It's best to shut up because, knowing Kat, she'll just up and walk away.

"*Anyway.* Where was I? Oh yeah—so Sheila was dumb and crazy and followed my dad all around with brownies and movie tickets, begging him to go out with her, so he finally said yes. She was always buying me and Charles stuff, clothes and toys and things—but I knew right away she was loony tunes. She was always screaming about something or crying for no reason. My dad asked her to move in, and she'd do stuff like that—burn a lasagna and then smash the dish and mope about it all day. And she *loved* Charles—she was batshit for Charles like you would not believe. It's probably because she couldn't have kids of her own. That's pretty common with fat ladies, you know. Anyway, she just oohed and aahed over him. Like he was some kind of angel or something. Gross."

She leans over and spits in the sink. Other things too: Sheila was horribly lazy and she didn't have any friends. A Sheila-shaped crater started to grow in the couch. She'd watch show after show and stare with her mouth slack, like it was real life and not TV. A week would go by and she'd do nothing, not a thing. Dishes would pile up in the sink and there'd be a greasy gleam to her hair. Other times she'd bolt out of her stupor and shout, "Everybody up! Let's go!" waving a mop around like some crazed majorette. There was a mouse that lived under the sink—they could hear it at night rustling through the trash—but Sheila said, "No way, José," and set up camp with a mallet and some cheese. No one bothered to stick around and watch—not even Charles, who lives for that kind of thing—because what was she gonna do? Hammer it to death? But later, who knows what time, they woke up to pounding and pounding and pounding. She couldn't hit it just once. She had to smash the thing into the floor. Even Charles was grossed out.

Then, suddenly, there's a place near the fridge that Kat is staring into, and Nenny knows she's not in the room anymore. Nenny, the kitchen, the house, all of it, have been sucked into some swirling black hole. Everyone knows memory is like that. Memory is a flood that overwhelms you. It crashes through windows and topples over walls, sweeps you away in a tide of furniture, photos, clothes you kind of hate, animals struggling to breathe.

"There were these kittens," Kat starts, but stops there.

"Kittens?" Nenny ventures. She's not heard anything about kittens before.

"Yeah," Kat says and looks at Nenny for the first time in a long time. Everywhere she's sixteen except her eyes. "Anyway." She turns back to the sink but doesn't spit this time. She doesn't really have to. "I'm glad she's dead." The house is quiet again. Nenny can hear the blood moving in her ears.

The rest Nenny finds out, but only slowly, over the years, because that's the way some stories go.

—⁓—

In June of 1984, Citrus Valley Community Hospital's board of directors voted unanimously to suspend a hiring freeze because, it turned out, they were dangerously understaffed. Patients were being left to die in the halls, nurses' stations were abandoned half the day. There was no one to run labs, change sheets, draw blood. And so on. Among the new hires were Sheila Collins, ER nurse, and Rick Wallace, respiratory therapist. They met at an all-staff training, and from then on Sheila pursued him like a hound. Whether or not he pursued her back is the only part of the story that remains unclear.

Boxes of donuts. Seven-layer nacho dip. Meatloaf or casserole at least once a week. Some Silly Putty and stickers because she knew he had kids. And what was he supposed to do? His wife had left, or anyway they weren't together anymore, so whatever walls he had built were wearing pretty thin.

Within a month she'd moved in. She wasn't exactly his type. Other women, including his wife, were all narrow and tall. They had wrists like thin branches and careful, sculpted cheeks. Their breasts were tender swollen dollops, their sweat smelled of sweet turning lime. They smoked pot, they did macramé, they believed in animal spirits and the energy of the third eye. They were happy to make love in abandoned warehouses, on piles of quilts, in the back seat of his car. They were angels, rising and falling each time they breathed.

Not Sheila. Sheila lay beneath him shivering like a frightened animal whenever they made love. She'd never smoked pot, had asthma, wore scrubs and housecoats, couldn't see without her goddamn glasses, had handwriting like a six-year-old's, periods that crippled her and gave her the shits for days, a bum shoulder, failing hips, weak knees. Sometimes all she did was cry. She was prone to incomprehensible fits of rage, tearing through the house with murderous intent. Once, Charles found some kittens at school, nestled in the outside trash. He brought them home cupped in his shirt, trembling with the fragile weight of the things, but Sheila said, "Kittens? No way." She filled a bucket with water, and that was the end of that.

What then must Rick feel, now that she's dead? Discreetly, Nenny watches him when he gets home, watches as he comes in and sets down the mail. He glances at the obituary on the table, which Mom had clipped and laid there. Nenny watches as he reads. She waits for something, anything, a headshake, a sigh. But he just sets the article back down and pours himself his evening glass of wine. He takes his shoes off at the bottom of the stairs and goes to change out of his scrubs. At dinner, no one says anything about it, not even Kat. They do the dishes, watch TV, get ready for bed. Still nothing, not a word, no sign that there'd once been a woman named Sheila and she'd—

Except, maybe, for this: in the morning, Nenny sees the obituary, covered in coffee grounds and part of a banana peel and bits of scrambled egg, crumpled up and soggy in the trash.

Tell It to Me Slowly

Boots is having her ninth birthday party at Shakey's Pizza, and Rick drives Nenny because he's going to San Bernardino and Shakey's is on the way. There's a house in San Bernardino that he owns and rents out, and sometimes it requires repairs. Rick and Nenny don't spend much time together, which is fine with Nenny and probably fine with Rick. Here's the thing: he's not a jerk, he's just, like, not nice. Not mean, but you know—not nice. He's the kind of grown-up who can't relate to kids, or be bothered to learn how. Most grown-ups will at least try, asking you about your friends or what you're learning in school. It's transparent, and boring, and dumb, but at least they try. Not Rick. It's obvious he thinks of childhood, the state of it, as something to be got through, something to begrudgingly endure—that maybe once Nenny's grown they might have some stuff in common, they might even get along, but for now let's just get this whole thing over with: your adolescence, your youth.

Which is to say: it's something of an awkward drive. A big quiet fills the car, practically sprawling across the seats. It's clear Rick wants to ask her things, ask about her life, if only for something to say—but he doesn't know how. Nenny thinks to ask about Gramma B but stays quiet, staring out the window instead. They drive down Dearborn, which is apparently the slowest street in the world, excruciatingly full of stop signs and red lights. Finally, Rick can't take it anymore and turns the radio on.

It's the oldies station. The DJ's name is Stutterin' Stan, or anyway that's what he goes by, *St-St-St-Stan!!!*, which is probably pretty insulting to people who actually stutter. He's annoying, for sure, but better than sitting in silence with Rick.

"N-n-n-next up! The Z-Z-Zombies!" It's a song Nenny's heard before. It starts with a confident bassline like a man strolling into a room, then a quick exhale, a sound like *t-ah* to follow the rolling bass. The voice, when it comes, is eerie and slow, like singing from the bottom of a well. *It's the ti-ime of the season*...She's heard this song before—everybody has. It's always in movies about the sixties, played over scenes of teenagers smoking drugs or young men marching off to war. It's a haunting song, heavy with mood. It's one of those songs that creeps up on you, hiding its intentions in cheesy organ riffs and layered harmonies. Nenny can't tell if she loves it or hates it—it's that kind of song.

"This song reminds me of Windsor," Rick says, out of nowhere, which is maybe an inappropriate and gross thing to say. Like, what are you even talking about? But when Nenny looks at him, it's clear he's not really talking to her at all. He taps out the rhythm on the steering wheel, whistles along. The thing about grown-ups—or, heck, even just other people—is that they spend a lot of time talking, but it's not to you; it's to themselves or something else entirely, something not even in the room.

Mysteries abound when you are young. Some unravel and reveal themselves over the course of your lifetime, but most remain unresolved. What was it, for example, that dissolved between Windsor and Rick? When Windsor comes over, their interactions are friendly and polite, as if the decision to end their marriage involved little more than a handshake and a mutual agreement to walk away. It's a kind of measured, mature interaction worlds away from what passes between Mom and Dad. Dad drops them home at the end of his visits and never, ever comes to the door. A number of his sentences begin "Tell your mother..." as if he can't just pick up the phone and tell her himself. To conjure Mom and Dad engaged in polite, adult conversation—to think of them sharing a handshake or a *hug*—is like trying to rearrange the contours of the universe. It simply cannot be done.

When they get to Shakey's, Rick says, "Okay, see you at five!" all cheerful like a normal person, like he doesn't spend most of his time somewhere between grumpy and annoyed. Guess that's the power of music for you.

The pizza parlor is jangly with sounds and lights. It's early afternoon on a Saturday, kids in soccer uniforms chasing each other around, their parents sitting together and sipping beer. Loud music, the smell of pizza, cars looping a racetrack on a giant TV—but really, the details are inconsequential, because Nenny won't remember any of it: not Boots's boisterous public-school friends, not the pizza, not the gifts, not the candles or the cake, if that was the party where some girl puked in the bathroom or if any of them cried. It's a pretty standard birthday party, as far as birthday parties go.

She will, though, remember that song, the ghostly voice and driving in the car with Rick. Not right away, but she'll remember it. It'll be one of those strange, belated memories that everyone has, like looking behind you and remembering something you didn't even know was there.

Let Down

A few Saturdays later Windsor comes to take Charles and Kat to the county fair. She was supposed to come last weekend; she didn't. It's impossible to know what happened, because Kat didn't say, just slammed the phone down and stormed upstairs. Later, though, Nenny overheard her on the phone—"I hate him. He's a pig."—so she guesses it has something to do with Gabe.

Now Nenny and Charles are in the living room, otherwise ignoring each other while they read. Mom announced a gardening day, and everyone else is outside, except Kat, who's still upstairs. Nenny's on the Baby-Sitters Club #5 again, *Dawn and the Impossible Three,* because she forgot the newest one at Dad's. That's another thing about divorce: you pack things and forget things and lose things all the time. There's a trail of your stuff like crumbs wherever you go.

It's impossible to concentrate anyways. Nenny knows Charles is still angry, even a week later, his leg bouncing as he testily flips a page. And why shouldn't he be? His mom made a promise that she didn't keep. Anyone would be mad. It occurs to

Nenny that there's going to be a fight, and she's not about to stick around for that. No way. She'll change for gardening day and join the others outside.

But halfway up the stairs the doorbell rings, and there's no time to make it all the way. Charles answers the door, and Nenny is stuck on the middle landing. She ducks quick and hugs the wall.

Though she can't see it happening, Nenny is still pained by Charles and Windsor's exchange. She hears Windsor's bracelets as Charles opens the door. Windsor says, "Hi, baby!" then there's a punctuated pause as she registers his mood. Silence, some whispered words, and Nenny pictures Windsor kneeling before Charles, begging forgiveness with her hands on his shoulders, with her shamed and supplicant eyes. Nenny can't help it: she steals a glance. She leans over and peeks quickly through the banister bars, catching a fast glimpse of Windsor's face. She looks exhausted—tumbled around and worn-out, with dark circles under her eyes and a pale, sagging quality to her skin. Nenny shrinks back. An excruciating amount of time passes. This isn't the first time that Windsor has failed to come. In fact, it seems like it happens every couple of weeks. Eventually, though, Charles must decide that he doesn't want to bear a grudge, it's not worth it, because finally Nenny hears the unmistakable sound of Windsor pulling him in for a hug. Nenny stays where she is, pressed to the wall, until she hears them go outside. Charles opens the back door and yells, "We're leaving now!" and Windsor laughs and says, "Honey, that's not polite." Nenny exhales only when she's sure they're outside.

But she doesn't get up right away. She clutches her book and hugs her knees and sits for a minute on the midway stairs. She knows what it's like to anticipate something, then to have your hope shrivel like a deflating balloon. Every time she goes to Dad's she expects something will have changed, that maybe this time he'll ask how she is, if she's happy, if anything's wrong, but he never does. He's so whacked and floating in his own world of grades and naps and dumb historical facts. The house could be on fire and he'd just sit there, with his cup of coffee and his stack of papers and his pile of red pens.

Then again, he always shows up. He's never *not* shown up. That's a different kind of disappointment entirely.

Geode

IF YOU think it isn't lame to have gardening day while your step-brother and stepsister are at the fair—well, you're wrong. It sucks. Well, maybe it doesn't suck, but it hardly compares to the county fair. There's an ancient curse on the fair because it was built on an Indian burial ground (it's true, ask anyone), but besides that they've got a petting zoo and a carousel and fried Twinkies and music shows. Nenny knows because the newspaper is always filled with giant ads.

But gardening isn't really even gardening, just pulling up a bunch of weeds. Mom says they're "prepping the soil," but Nenny's not stupid: they're weeding. Weeds are called weeds because they're stubborn as heck, snapping away from their own roots like *Nice try, sucker!* They're relentless in their will to live. There's pill bugs everywhere and daddy longlegs that scurry across your patch of dirt, and occasionally you'll find weird, oblong pebbles that turn out to be some cat's turd.

That said, Mom did buy them their own gardening gloves—Nenny's are the color of a ripe peach—and give them each a little tool, like a screwdriver with a fork on the end, and there's lemonade on the table, and Rick promised pizza for dinner if they pitch in and don't complain. There are worse things in this world than gardening day.

Rick's up on the hill, hacking away at a tangle of branches and weeds, and Mom and Tiny are working together over by the fence. Even from here you can tell he's blathering on about nothing. Bubbles is off in the corner, sifting through dirt, and Cosby sleeps in a spot of shade by the pool. Nenny puts on her gloves and sets to work, making little piles as she digs: over here the broken weeds, over here—to show Mom—the weeds with their roots, over here a small pile of stones. *What if* this *is an ancient burial ground?* she thinks, spiking her forked tool into the earth. Even if it wasn't a burial ground, probably an Indian was here at some point, a long time ago, before it was a weed-strewn patch of dirt next to a pool, and before that an orange grove stretching to the mountains, and before that who knows. She pictures an Indian girl weeding in her mother's yard, then thinks wait, did Indians have weeds? Then thinks they probably ate them, then thinks that's messed up—is that messed up? By now her piles are more weeds than stones. The Indians who used to live here were called the Serranos. Every year the fourth graders at school research a California mission and build a model out of sticks or sugar cubes, and every year it's always the same—tiny Indians in the mission gardens, raking soil or planting seeds or forming bricks, or else praying with some priest in a courtyard somewhere, the feeling one of peaceful camaraderie, of a fair and equitable and friendly exchange, and every year, walking through the cafeteria where the models are on display, Nenny thinks, *Yeah, right.* Everyone knows the Indians were slaves.

Next year, she thinks, *when I'm in fourth grade, my model's gonna tell the truth,* and pictures sugar cubes specked with painted blood and little figurine faces twisted with rage.

"Hey!" Bubbles suddenly shouts. "Look what I found!"

He's still in the corner of the yard where he started. He thrusts a rock into the air and shouts again, "Look!"

"What is it, honey?" Mom calls back, and he runs to her, the rock held before him like a precious stone. "Look, look!" he keeps saying, even though she's already looking.

Nenny goes to see what all the fuss is about. She and Tiny and Mom stand in a tight horseshoe around Bubbles, who holds out his treasure. It looks like what it is: a rock.

"What is it, sweetie?" Mom asks again, gently, careful not to deflate his enthusiasm over an ordinary backyard stone. Bubbles stares wide-eyed at the rock, his hand quivering.

"I think it's a *geode,*" he says, the full weight of his wonder polishing the word.

Everyone's quiet. "A what?" Mom finally asks.

"A *geode.*" He sounds like Indiana Jones, stumbling upon some amazing discovery in a cavern somewhere.

Mom blinks. She's trying to conceal the irritation creeping into her voice. There's still a lot of weeding to do. "Honey, what's a geode?"

"What is it?" Tiny repeats, and everyone stares at Bubbles, who stares back.

"It's a rock with diamonds inside," he says. "You crack it open and there's diamonds inside." It looks like a regular rock— rounder than average, maybe, a little smoother, but there's nothing special about it, nothing really to distinguish it from any other rock in the yard.

"Honey, I'm not sure..." They all stare at Mom as she

searches for words. It's classic Mom: if she has to let you down, she wants to let you down easy. "I don't think geodes grow around here."

"Grow?" Bubbles says. "Geodes don't grow. They just are."

"You know what I mean, honey. I don't think this is geode territory."

Nenny and Tiny look back and forth from Mom to Bubbles, Bubbles to Mom. Bubbles stares at his rock for a good minute, looking like he might cry, which is maybe why Mom adds brightly, "But who knows! Maybe it is a geode. What do I know about rocks?"

That's enough for Bubbles. He breaks up the circle and runs to the base of the hill. "Rick!" he calls up. "I found a geode!"

"Oh yeah?" Rick says, still shoveling. There's sweat soaking through his shirt, and you can tell he doesn't give two farts about the stone.

"Yeah!" Bubbles shouts. Rick doesn't say anything else, just keeps shoveling, so Bubbles shouts, "Can we crack it open?"

Rick pauses and blinks and looks over at Mom, who just shrugs. "Sure," Rick says. "Later. After we're done."

It's a pseudo yes, but a yes is a yes, and Bubbles pumps his fist and runs back to his corner by the fence. There's no way around it: Bubbles is a strange kid. It's impossible to tell if he's a genius or just plain dumb. His grades are horrible and he hates to read and he often seems baffled by simple tasks, like buttoning his own pants, but then again is able to succinctly explain things no one else can, like how come in *Back to the Future* Marty's photo begins to disappear. ("Time's folding in on itself," he'd said, "making things erase.") Now he paces back and forth in the corner of the yard, cradling the rock close. Occasionally another rock catches his attention, and he'll pick it up, examine it, but ultimately toss it aside. From where Nenny's sitting, they all look the same—boring backyard stones.

Bubbles must get an idea, though, because suddenly he abandons his post and runs inside. If anyone notices, they don't seem to care. A few minutes later, he comes back with one of the encyclopedia books. She doesn't have to guess what volume it is.

Nenny sidles over, takes off her gloves, and pretends to sip some lemonade. He doesn't notice her. "What're you reading?" she finally asks. Bubbles isn't like Charles; she doesn't have to worry about pissing him off.

He taps the page but doesn't look up. "I told you," he says, turning the book so she can see.

Told me what? she thinks and starts to read. "A geode is a round, hollow rock containing a cavity lined with mineral matter." Mineral matter must mean diamonds. She glances up to compare the photos to his rock, which he helpfully holds out so she can take a closer look, though he obviously doesn't want her to touch it. The shape is basically the same, although the texture looks different. The geodes in the book are all bumpy and gross, like blistered or diseased skin, but Bubbles's rock is as smooth as, well, stone. It's a little *too* perfectly shaped, too egglike, too good to be true.

She shrugs. "Could be one, I guess."

"I know," Bubbles says, his voice filled with wondrous hope. He holds the rock close to his face, rotating it in his palm. What does he think is gonna happen? He'll crack it open and there will be diamonds inside, precious enough to sell for millions? And he'll take the money and what? Buy a house big enough to fit them all? Everyone gets their own room? Cool appliances like on *The Jetsons*? Soda pop fountains, slides instead of stairs?

Tiny comes over because Tiny can't stay away. "There's diamonds in there?" He points a cartoonishly rigid finger at the stone.

"Maybe," Bubbles says, a strangely tempered response. "Probably."

Tiny starts one of his stories. "Manny Hernandez, his dad drives a truck, an' one time he was driving in Youtah and the wheels got flatted, an' when he got out to 'vestigate, there was a *snake* wrapped in the wheels." He spreads his arms. "A big one."

"That's nice," Bubbles says, and Nenny rolls her eyes.

"Mom!" Tiny shouts. "Can we crack open the geome now?" It sounds like *cwack* when he says it.

"Ge*ode*," Bubbles corrects.

There's a pause because either Mom didn't hear or she's deferring to Rick, who's still on the hill. Tiny and Nenny look at Bubbles, who's quiet and probably hoping Rick has overheard and will intervene. But Rick doesn't, either overhear or intervene—there's a tree stump the size of a small beast embedded in the hill, Rick digging trenches around its roots with the fervency and the fever of a man who's dug trenches before.

"Rick said we'll break it open later," Bubbles eventually says, his enthusiasm eroded a bit.

But later's a long time away. They eat a few crackers and drink lemonade, then wander back to work. Bubbles stays in the shade, reading about geodes. The long haze of afternoon slouches across the sky. Nenny finishes pulling weeds from her patch of dirt. She counts thirty-five unbroken ones, uses her rake tool to smooth the soil, neatly organizes her pile of stones. It's time for the flowers. This is Nenny's favorite part: moving flowers around, deciding where they'll go. She takes three containers of pansies and four alyssums and three marigolds and carefully carries them to her spot. She spreads the alyssum packs into a careful arc, then changes her mind and does alyssum, pansy, alyssum, pansy, with three marigold packs arranged in the center. For the first time all day, Cosby rouses herself. She struggles against her own weight and near-atrophied limbs, sniffs for a minute near the edge of the grass, squats rigidly, then takes a massive, man-sized dump on the lawn.

Whatever focus the day had held has evaporated like a spell. Tiny plucks dandelions and makes wishes while Bubbles sits under the unfinished patio roof, no longer reading, just holding his rock and occasionally glancing up the hill at Rick. With meticulous care, as if this were a lasting endeavor, as if these dumb flowers won't all be dead in a number of weeks, Nenny plants her flowers and with her own stack of worthless stones makes a perfect circle clustered around the marigolds in the middle.

Finally, Rick comes down the hill and slaps his gloves against his thigh, lowers himself into a chair, and takes long, hearty gulps from a giant glass of lemonade. Bubbles sits beside him, clutching his stone.

"Um, Rick?" he ventures, like poking a sleeping bear. "Do you think we could break open my geode now?"

Rick doesn't even look at him, just grunts, "I said pizza first," then empties another glass. Rick cannot abide the harmless sentimentality of some boys. It's clear this has nothing to do with pizza or his sun-drenched fatigue and everything to do with some idea of what it means to be a man.

Why doesn't Bubbles just break the rock open on his own? He's almost eleven years old, for criminy's sake—it's not like he's never swung a hammer before. Clearly he could break the thing open without smashing his fingers or toes.

The answer to that is simple, though: it's not about the rock anymore. Watching Bubbles watch Mom and Rick, tracking them with his sad, quiet eyes, any moron can see it's about something else.

The afternoon is edging on dusk when Kat and Charles and Windsor return. Charles slams open the back door and runs around the table, swinging an inflatable mallet over his head. Kat goes to Rick to show him her new ring, a little silver sliver on her pinky, and Mom says, "Hi, how was it?" and stands to give Windsor a hug. Rick says, "That's a nice ring," though you can tell it's kind of crappy and cheap, even from here, and Kat smiles and Windsor says, "We had so much fun!" like she didn't expect to, like she's surprised.

"Bubbles found a ge-ome!" Tiny says, tugging on her sleeve. "Over there in the yard!"

"A ge-ome?" Windsor says. "What's that?"

"It's a rock, an' when you smash it, it's got diamonds inside!"

"Diamonds!" Windsor exclaims. "Real diamonds?" And Tiny nods vigorously. She doesn't look tired anymore. She looks refreshed, calm in a way she wasn't this morning, somehow more put together after a long day at the fair. Thing is, you can be cursed and not cursed at the same time. Just because you have troubles doesn't mean you're troubled all the time.

"Yeah huh, real diamonds!" Tiny says, holding the arm of Windsor's chair and bouncing on his toes.

"Yeah, right." Kat snorts.

"That's great," Windsor says, turning to Bubbles. "May I see it?"

Bubbles hesitates only briefly before placing it in her hand. He's been silent and sheepish this whole time, his chin tucked into his chest, the rock hand-cradled in his lap, a fragile thing like a baby bird. But he hands it to her anyway, because it's clear she won't drop it or make fun of him or snort and roll her eyes.

"This is a very nice rock," Windsor says, carefully turning it over in her palm. In case you're a moron, it should be noted that that's a really nice thing to do: tell some kid that the rock he found is great, even though it isn't and, also, he's not even your kid. Everyone's kind of quiet for a minute, maybe regretting how they're always laughing at Bubbles and dismissing him when he doesn't deserve it. He's the nicest one of them all.

"All right, get the hammer," Rick finally says.

"Really?" Bubbles says.

"Sure," Rick says. "It's in the garage." He puts on his hat and stands up.

"Yeah!" Charles yells. "Smash, smash!"

Okay, so say they crack the thing open. Say Bubbles gets the hammer and everybody stands up from their chairs and follows him over to the pavement by the pool, and they all gather around him in the rising dusk, no pushing, no shoving, no snorting or jokes. Say they circle around him respectfully, quietly, like this is some kind of ceremony and they're all equally invested and involved—what do you think happens? Honestly: what do you think happens when Bubbles brings the hammer up over his head—arms trembling with all his mustered strength, the focus on his face like something pinned there—and then brings the hammer down and smashes it open? Honestly, seriously, what do you think is inside that stone?

Off-Limits

Is IT true of every house that some things are off-limits? Nenny thinks about this sometimes: what do other families *not* say? Because there's plenty they don't talk about at 926 Kensington Drive, that's for sure. *Welcome to our home! Please leave your muddy shoes and most topics of conversation outside.*

For example: they don't talk about Gramma B or what happens when you die. They don't talk about the people who have died, other grandparents or Uncle Max's wife. Puberty is a freakish mystery hidden on a shelf. Nenny can talk about her feelings, but only with Mom, and she has to try not to cry if she does. If she cries and Rick overhears, he'll say, "Knock it off," like she's crying just to annoy him. Which of course is totally messed up but will make a kind of sense in the long run, as she ages and certain things are revealed: Rick's dad smashing dishes and shattering bottles and breaking doors. They don't talk about that stuff either.

The biggest thing they don't talk about, though, the greatest silence in the room, is Vietnam.

They dine around and do chores around and argue around

and sometimes play around Vietnam. Vietnam sits at every meal, jungle-breathed and bleary-eyed, sprawled across their plates. Vietnam is a hungry dog shivering at the foot of the bed. Vietnam is the constant thing between them. Vietnam, ugly and childish and hiding and damned. It slithers the hallways and skulks the stairs. Vietnam lurks in every room, laughing in the dark, mashing hot paws into its own shit and piss and blood, probing its own wretched body for sores.

Semper Fi, Assholes

WHAT NENNY knows about the war in Vietnam could fit on the back of a napkin. Not a big napkin either, but one of those small napkins old ladies use when they play bridge.

1. Vietnam is a country in Asia. Asia is one of the seven continents, probably the biggest in the world, though sometimes Nenny gets confused. Is Russia part of Asia? Because Russia's pretty big.

2. There was a war in Vietnam. Supposedly a really bad one because no one will talk about it, and if it is mentioned, Mom grows quiet like when people are unsure what to say — though what makes one war worse than another escapes Nenny, and always will.

3. The war in Vietnam happened a *long* time ago, before Nenny was even born. Back then Mom's hair went down to her waist, and Dad had peach fuzz blooming all over

his cheeks. They weren't even married yet, just two kids eyeing each other in the halls at school.

4. Rick was a soldier in Vietnam—but before you get any crazy ideas, he was a *medic*. That means he was saving people, not killing them. Duh.

Here's how it went: There was a war happening in Vietnam, and Rick probably saw it on the news and said, "You know what? Those people need saving." So he signed up for the war, and they gave him a medicine bag and one of those white coats that doctors wear, and he went over there and waited quietly and patiently in his tent until someone got hurt, and then he bandaged them up, put them on a helicopter, and said nice things like "You get on home, soldier." He went back into his tent until someone else got hurt, and then he did it all over again. If they ever had to march anywhere, he always marched at the back of the line and his white coat made him stand out and the enemy never tried to shoot at him so he was never in danger and he was always fine. The end.

Except that's not the end, because one day Charles discovers an old can of shoe polish and a bunch of other junk out in the garage. When Nenny finds him, half an hour later, he's smeared polish under his eyes and ripped the sleeves off his camo tee. He's Ramboed bits of cloth around his head and wrists, and is busy at work with some duct tape and an old wrapping paper tube.

"What're you doing?" Nenny asks, because even though she could give two farts, she hates to not be involved.

"Private Joker! You will speak when spoken to!" He doesn't even look at her when he shouts. She rolls her eyes and goes to the freezer for a Popsicle. She sits on a stool, watching him.

"Is that a gun?" she asks, because they're not allowed to play with guns. Indiana Jones whip, Nerf rocket launchers, fine—but not guns.

"*This,*" Charles says, hoisting it up with pride, "is a special-issue sniper rifle, the third-deadliest conventional weapon after the laser bomb." It looks like what it is: a bunch of taped-together trash. He puts the scope up to his eye and scans along an imaginary horizon somewhere outside the open garage door. "Charlie doesn't stand a chance!"

Whoa. Charlie? Who the heck is Charlie? Some kind of other version of himself? Charles versus Charlie in the ultimate fight? Cause that would be—what's the word? Super deep. Nenny's a little amazed. "Charlie?" she asks, wondering if his secret genius is about to be revealed.

"The gooks, stupid."

"The gooks?"

"The Viet*cong.*" He lowers his gun and looks at her like she's the biggest idiot that ever lived.

"What? Are you playing Vietnam?"

"I'm not playing Vietnam. I *am* Vietnam." He lifts the gun again and lets off a few imaginary rounds. "Semper fi, assholes."

Forget about the fact that swearing is forbidden, let alone guns. "Charles," Nenny says, with special holy emphasis, "you can't play Vietnam."

"Why in the hell not?" he says back.

Nenny glances over her shoulder, as if being watched. "Because your dad was in Vietnam, stupid."

Charles shrugs. "I'll tell 'em I'm playing family history." He lays the gun on the workbench and starts adding details with a marker.

Nenny watches him, her head spinning. Something feels

trampled, like just by talking about it they're kicking dirt onto someone's grave.

And then an important fact occurs to her, and she feels it's worth mentioning if only in order to prove what a complete moron Charles is. "Besides," she says, drawing out her words, "Rick was a medic. He didn't kill anybody. He didn't even have a gun."

"Are you cracked?" His face is sharp. "It was a war. Everyone killed everyone, stupid."

Now he's clearly lying. "Oh, okay. Everyone killed everyone. Sure. And, um, how do you know that, by the way? Did you make a cardboard time machine too?"

"Haven't you ever seen *Platoon*?" he says. She looks at him and he looks back, both of them with eyebrows raised. "*Full Metal Jacket*? *Apocalypse Now*?" She keeps her face passive and her arms crossed, because Charles is an imbecile and she knows she's not wrong.

"Whatever." He shrugs and picks up a cardboard walkie-talkie. And then, like that, he shuts something on her, one of his inside doors, and it's clear he's back in the jungle of his own mind, far away from Nenny.

"Private Joker! Do you copy?!!" he screams into his walkie-talkie. He takes some imaginary shots, gets pegged by a stray bullet, clutches his gut, and tumbles out the garage door.

Idiot, Nenny thinks and goes back inside to read. She finds, though, that she can't concentrate. *That can't be true*, she thinks. Rick was a medic, and medics didn't kill people—they saved people. That was their job; that was the whole point.

Still, she suddenly finds that she's not so sure.

Platoon

As IT happens, Dad is *obsessed* with war. He owns all the essential nonfiction books about war, books with titles like *To Hell and Back* and *The Guns of August* and *Bury My Heart at Wounded Knee*, and at one time or another has read the novels too. He has subscriptions to *After the Battle* and *Field Artillery* magazines.

Thing is, Dad's never actually been to war, and never will. If you ever hear someone say "He's just not cut out for it" and you're not sure who "he" is, now you know: they're talking about Nenny's dad. His greatest sadness in life, other than splitting from Mom, is that he'll never go to war. He'll never even see the inside of a bunker, other than some dorky fake one at a county museum somewhere, because apparently when Dad turned eighteen, his doctor said, "Ho, boy! Not with your asthma!" and stamped his card 4-F, which is armyspeak for "Unable to serve."

But anyone with half a brain (or with a dad who's half-obsessed) knows that 4-F might put an end to your ambitions of seeing the theater but it can't ever squelch your God-given right to own obscure manuals, decommissioned grenades, rusty helmets, boot liners, medals and backpacks and ponchos and canteens, even a creepy gas mask that's starting to mold.

Movies too. Dad owns all the movies too.

—◆—

Saturday, and Dad's grading papers in the other room. This means they can basically do whatever they want. Bubbles is out front, playing Legos. Tiny's in his fort—first thing he does at Dad's is build a fort—but Nenny doesn't have time for games.

"Let's watch a movie," she says to Tiny, because since Charles's revelation it's all she thinks about. She doesn't want to think about it, but she can't help it. It's been a week, and every day, several times a day, she can hear Charles say, "Everyone killed everyone, stupid," and each time her mind grows foggy and her stomach flips. She wants desperately to believe he's wrong, but she's just not sure anymore.

"*Ernest Goes to Camp!*" Tiny chirps from his fort.

"No, not *Ernest Goes to Camp*." His disappointment is palpable. She runs her fingers along the cassette spines. Hundreds of movies line the shelves, literally hundreds. War paraphernalia's not Dad's only problem. The other is that whenever a movie is released on tape, he's got to have it. There are so many tapes he has to keep adding new shelves.

Scarface, Moby Dick, Casablanca, Tarzan the Ape Man, Tarzan Finds a Son, Tarzan's New York Adventure...and then she sees it, and when she does, something inside her sinks. A man—you can't even see his face—kneels with his arms outstretched, as if he's reaching for or calling out to God. Except he's covered in blood, and there are men with guns behind him, so it's hard to believe that it's some kind of prayer. There was a part of her that hoped

Dad wouldn't have the movie, that she could just carry on in blissful ignorance—but the fact that it's here has all the crushing and twisted complications of fate. She *has* to watch it now. She doesn't have a choice.

"How about this one?" she says, trying to conceal her nerves.

"What is it?" Tiny says, popping out of his fort. He walks over and snatches the cassette from her hand. He seems completely disinterested—it's hard to compete with Ernest—but then he flips it over and gasps.

"This movie's rated R," he whispers, his eyes bulging from his skull.

"So?" Nenny shrugs, trying her best to be cavalier.

"We're not allowed!"

This is an easy enough problem to fix. *"Dad! Can we watch a movie?"*

She's already sliding the cassette from its sleeve because she knows what the answer will be.

"Yes! Please don't shout! I'm grading papers!" Dad shouts.

"See?" Nenny says, putting the tape in the VCR. The machine whirs to life.

At first it's pretty straightforward. Charlie Sheen gets off a helicopter in what is obviously supposed to be Vietnam. He's clearly the new guy in the battalion and doesn't (thankfully) look anything like Rick. Rick is lanky and tall without a hair on his head, and Charlie Sheen is, well, Charlie Sheen. "Welcome to the 'Nam!" some guy shouts and claps him on the back. Charlie Sheen does a sheepish, aw-shucks kind of face, and off they go.

Nenny scans the screen. She's waiting for the medic to appear—white coat gleaming in a sea of green. Or maybe just a Red Cross medicine bag. But when the medic does show—five minutes in—he's just like every other guy: rugged and calloused and wearing that awful, filthy green. So there it is. Charles was right. She feels like she might be sick.

"Can we watch the other one now?" Tiny whines. He's lolling like a dead tongue out the door of his fort, sprawled and arm-splayed because this movie will be the death of him. "Shhhh-hhh," Nenny says. It's the sustained, soft *shhhhhhh* of *It's all right, it's okay*. Who knows if she's comforting and quieting him or comforting and quieting herself.

Just to be clear, *Platoon* is NOT *Ernest Goes to Camp*. It is a gruesome, gruesome film. Scarred, crude men fight for power in their ranks. They curse one another and betray one another without blinking an eye. They talk about whores and pussy and fuck you fuck this fuck that like it's anything else. They're alive with ants and rage. Charlie Sheen cowers in the brush, crouched under a sheet and soaked to the bone, and the shadows of the Vietcong, bodies materializing from the night woods, and the drumbeat, and the heartbeat, and the drum.

There is a knife to Nenny's throat. Rick did two tours in Vietnam—two tours. Each tour lasts a year, she thinks, and to imagine this kind of life, day after day after day. As she watches the movie, all of the soldiers become Rick—Rick grazed in the neck by a bullet, Rick facedown in the mud, Rick screaming and panicked in the heat of a firefight. Rick is all of Bravo Company, an entire battalion, a whole infantry, and every other soldier who ever stepped foot in Vietnam. He storms a village, kicks over rice sacks, shoots a pig, screams in some woman's face, yanks children by the arm, and then slams the butt of his rifle into a one-legged man's cheek, over and over and over again, until the man's skull explodes. "You see that head fucking come apart, man?"

Platoon is not a bulb going off. It's an entire stadium, suddenly lit, flooded with awful light.

Rick is all of them—each murderous, wild, defiant, lonely, terrified one.

And he lives in Nenny's house.

And he sleeps right upstairs.

How to Think About Ghosts

First of all, forget about Casper. Casper's a freaking joke. Watch Casper and you're led to believe that death is some kind of *fun*. That once you lose your physical form it's all cuddly marshmallows floating around, cute as buttons, soft and wispy as clouds. That death is little more than an extension of a charmed and adorable life where occasionally, just for the hell of it, everyone breaks into song.

Nothing could be further from the truth.

Real ghosts reach through walls, and sometimes they don't have faces—just crisped slabs of flesh where their eyes and mouths should be. They certainly don't sing. They don't even moan like ghosts in other shows do. They're silent as holes, as muffled as desperate pleas to *go away, go away, go away*. Steer clear of the bathroom at night. Ghosts *love* the bathroom at night. They wait for you faceup and bleeding at the bottom of the tub, or still and searching in the mirror, looking into your face for glimpses of their own. They drag their bloodied limbs and broken flesh down darkened halls, and when their guts fall out, which their guts always do, real ghosts stand, night after night, at the top of the stairs, pushing what should not be out back in. There's no getting rid of real ghosts. There's no praying or begging or wishing real ghosts away. Distractions, pleas, bullets, napalm, years—your ghosts are here to stay.

Premonition

SOMETHING TERRIBLE is going to happen. Something awful and deadly is about to occur. This is less a fear than an absolute premonition. Fear rides high in the chest, nestles like a stone in the throat, but this? This is the oppressive, terrifying sensation of being watched, everything a beast with eyes.

In dreams, someone—nameless and faceless and without shape or voice—stands over Nenny's bed wielding an ax, and she wakes in the morning drenched in sweat. She looks at her siblings and involuntarily imagines them annihilated—Bubbles impaled by a bayonet, Tiny sliced apart, Charles knifed in the back, Kat riddled with wounds. She prays fervently because that's what she's been taught to do: *Hail Mary, full of grace, Hail Mary, full of grace, Hail Mary, Hail Mary, Hail Mary.* The other kids at school aren't even idiots now because the other kids aren't even there. Everyone else has melded into an indistinguishable mass. Three times Nenny tries to talk to Mom and three times the words snag tangled in her throat; three times *Mommy, I need help,* three times severed *Mommy, I'm scared,* and Mom in her own wordless cloud, distracted and overworked. Nenny cannot bear to look at Rick. If she looks at Rick, even a glance, then his secret will be revealed and he will expertly, coldly, and without mercy kill them all.

Boots is the only one who seems to notice that something is wrong.

"Are you okay?" she asks, afternoon sky, murky pool.

Nenny's brow furrows and her heart does a wrinkled flip. She loves Boots instantly then because she's even asked.

But Boots wouldn't understand. No one, anywhere, at any time, will ever understand.

Pressing

THURSDAY NIGHT, Mom's putting Nenny to bed. Time for only one question, and for Nenny it's the most pressing question of all.

"Mom...did Rick kill people in Vietnam?"

Mom sighs. "Oh, Nenny. That was a long time ago." Which is not an answer. She goes to the door and turns out the light. "It's time to go to sleep."

Go on, Nenny. Try to sleep.

Call It Love

NENNY'S NINTH birthday comes. There's the familiar white cake and the silly drawn-out song. At the end of the table, a little pile of gifts, and on the pile, the littlest of gifts, perched like a small bird at the top of a tree. The tag says, "To Nenny, From Rick." She did not expect a gift from him and looks at him for the first time all week.

"It's a locket," he says before she's even opened it. "I figured you could put a picture of Kirk Cameron in it or something."

What? Did he just—but how does he know? How does Rick know? That her love for Kirk Cameron is like having her heart pinched of blood and then dipped in gold? How could Rick possibly know?

Rick folds his napkin, sips his wine, folds his napkin again, but he won't look at her. Nenny realizes something then, and it's a strange flash that shifts the very walls of the room. *He's embarrassed*, she thinks. He's overcome by this simple exchange. It's as if he's not sure how to hold this thing he's got, this fragile, fledgling thing—call it affection, call it love.

A Sight to See

Is THIS it? Is this the impending terrible thing? Gramma B dies. It doesn't *feel* all that terrible. She wasn't Nenny's actual grandma, after all.

But what a strange, horrifying, lovely sight: to see Rick push his glasses up and pinch his tear ducts like some men do. What a thing, to watch him like this, to see him cry.

—⁊⁊—

After that, the fear recedes a little, like a retreating tide. Nenny will learn this over and over again throughout her life, how it comes and goes, the way that fear comes and goes.

Rhymes with "Boss"

WINDSOR LIVES in Apple Valley, which may as well be the moon. It's only an hour away but feels much farther. It's an endless drive of dust and dirt and stones. What separates their house from Charles and Kat's other house is a landscape so brown that it's greyed, frail trees struggling alone in barren fields, buildings with their windows knocked out, the stain of raunchy motels and tilting houses and wasted trailer parks. They are places where no one wants to live but that they desperately inhabit.

The whole family's driving up because small stories have been swirling around. Nothing concrete, but stories still: Charles told Bubbles, who let it slip, something about Gabe's collection of *Playboy* magazines, and Kat hates Gabe with a vehemence that could dissolve you. Who knows what he's done, but anyway something's fishy and Rick wants to check it out. He would never say as much, but Nenny's not stupid: they're doing recon.

Kat and Charles take the swivel seats; Nenny and the boys climb in the back. Supposedly they're taking Charles and Kat to Windsor's for the weekend and on the way hitting some desert zoo, but everyone knows this is a cover. Windsor usually comes to pick up Kat and Charles, and no way would Rick volunteer to drive there out of the kindness of his heart or to see some zoo.

"We're here!" Mom finally sings, then points out the window and cries, "How cute!" Nenny doesn't even have to look to know she's feeding them a line. The zoo parking lot is completely empty, and though there's a big OPEN sign, it's dangling at an angle like a wonky eye. Even the sign is looking for some better place to go.

"At least it's free," Rick says.

"What a steal," Charles mumbles as they get out of the car.

An old man comes out of the "office" and starts hobbling toward them across the lot. He looks as though he hasn't bathed, slept, changed his clothes, been outside, or seen another human being in about ten thousand years. Nenny imagines showing him a VCR and watching his head explode.

"Well, hell-oooooo!" he calls. He's lurching toward them like they're the long-lost relatives he's been searching for his whole life.

"Ew," Kat says but shuts it when Rick shoots her a look. The man's name tag says HOSS, and he looks about a billion years old: skin like a crumpled paper bag, every other tooth missing. His glasses are so scratched and dusty it's a wonder he can see at all.

"Hoss?" Tiny asks, pointing to the tag.

"Rhymes with 'boss'!" the guy says, clapping Tiny on the shoulder. Tiny beams. He's constantly falling for guys who have no actual authority: lifeguards at the YMCA, the security guard at the bank, anybody in a uniform. He wants to be everyone's sidekick. He's always hungry for some dorky hat, some crappy plastic badge.

Hoss offers them a tour, and Mom bugs her eyes like *Oooh, a tour!* The tour only goes to show what a crap hole the place is—not that they needed proof. Hoss leads them past lines of cages filled with listless, sick-looking lizards, all of them named: Mr. Scales, Mr. Scales Junior, Green Eyes, Wanda.

"Wanda?" Kat blurts, suddenly attentive.

"Yeah—after my ex-wife!" old Hoss cries, then starts heaving and coughing and slapping his knee. Boy, he's a real riot. Hoss is a downright clown.

"This one's dead," Charles announces, poking his finger into a cage. The lizard is belly-up, waxen, its mouth open and teeth exposed.

Hoss hunches down and leans in real close. It's clear the thing is long gone—there are ants already exploring its mouth. But Hoss just stands there, hands on his knees, peering into the cage. It occurs to Nenny that maybe he's seeing more than a dead lizard, maybe he's seeing something else, something only an old desert hermit could see—the face of God breaking through a cloud, angels in descent, that kind of thing.

But then he says, "I'll be damned. Sure is," and yanks it out of the cage. Then, unexpectedly, he chucks it as far as it will go. It makes a high, swift arc over the line of cages, landing with a dull thump in the far-off sand.

—◊—

The rest of the tour lasts about a century. Even Mom is visibly glad when it's over, though she thanks him profusely and presses a five-dollar bill into his hand. Tiny keeps shouting, "G'bye, Hoss! G'bye!" as Kat closes the van door. And of course old Hoss continues standing there, one hand up like *So long! See you next time!* He's probably standing there still, favoring that one leg, waving and waving goodbye.

Happy Trails

THE TRAILER park where Windsor lives in Apple Valley is called Happy Trails, but there's nothing happy about the place. There aren't even any trails, just rutted dirt roads. Trailer parks, you never know what you're gonna get. Gramma B's was manicured and pristine, each trailer with its own rock garden or collection of ceramic gnomes.

Happy Trails is different, though. There's not a decorative anything anywhere. It's the kind of place where men smoke on their porches, alone or in lonely groups, and kids kneel in the dirt lighting matches, watching them burn. A couple of girls walk barefoot in the road, and when they see the van, they giggle like it's some big secret, the van, this great divide. Mom starts to roll up her window but then stops, leaving it halfway. Other adults would roll the window all the way up, flick the visor down and pretend the sun was in their eyes, find some reason to not have to look at people who have a different kind of house or live a different kind of life. Not Mom. Mom treats everyone the same.

Windsor's standing on the porch when they pull up, as if waiting for them or waiting for something, anything, who knows. She starts waving high and big, like landing a rescue plane, a wide smile on her face, the tassels on her leather jacket swinging back and forth.

"There's your mom!" Mom says, waving back, though Windsor's only two feet away.

"Well, hiya!" Windsor calls. She and Mom always hug like old friends, which is odd when you think about it. "Where's my baby?" she coos, opening her arms for Charles. He doesn't even flinch, just goes right into the curve of her and lets himself be hugged, even hugs back.

"Hello, girl," she says to Kat, who steps forward into her embrace. She says hi to Rick, and they do this side-hug thing that's reserved but not without affection.

Windsor turns to Nenny and the boys. "Hi, guys, come on in. I've got brownies and lemonade. Tiny, you like brownies and lemonade?"

The inside of the trailer is damp and cool like the stifled gut of a cave. It's clean, but maybe not always, and furnished in a haphazard, piecemeal way: a fraying couch spruced up with some afghans, a few vases with fake roses here and there. The TV is on but muted. Matlock silently rattles his jowls. There are pictures of Kat and Charles everywhere, some the same as they have at home, others Nenny's never seen before. There's also photos of Gramma Sadie, their other grandma, who takes them to *The Nutcracker* every year and other places and events they loathe. There's a lot of photos of a lean, dull-eyed girl about Kat's age, who must be Becca. She's Gabe's daughter, and the only thing Nenny knows about her is that she has a tattoo and hates Gabe as much as Kat and Charles do. Nenny sometimes imagines Kat and Becca painting their nails and chewing gum and finding photos of Gabe and scratching out all the eyes.

"Gabe's at the store," Windsor says, as if they've come to see him, as if they're holding their breath.

"It looks nice in here, Windsor," Mom says. There's something phony in all of this, the whole thing—Windsor's outsized affection, the hugs, the small talk—as if with their subtle theatrics Mom and Windsor can deflate the terrible awkwardness in the room.

Nobody's sure what to do. The two moms chatter away about nothing while Rick listens politely, twirling his hat on his fingers. The kids kind of linger by the door, except Kat, who's in the kitchen getting brownies—which is, like, Kat helping without being asked? This is a historic moment. Someone should make a plaque.

The brownies are dusty, or anyway that's how they taste. Slowly the boys leak into the living room, and Kat starts flipping through a magazine. The grown-ups talk about the stupidest stuff, and Nenny briefly wonders if this is how they'll spend the rest of eternity: talking about nothing and waiting like broken glass.

Then a car door slams.

"There he is!" Windsor chirps, though not brightly enough to hide a slight crack in her voice. When Gabe walks in, Nenny realizes she'd been expecting a monster—barrel-chested and shirtless, with storms and the deaths of small children raging in his eyes. But he's not—he's just a wiry little flea of a man, with a push-broom moustache and glasses that take up half his face. Supposedly he's been at the store for nearly an hour, but he comes in with no bags.

"Well, howdy, all!" he crows, letting the screen door slam.

Windsor grows visibly tense. On the couch, Charles does and undoes the limbs of Megatron, his back to the door, elbow on Kat's knee. At home they hardly talk, but now they're practically snuggled up, neither of them looking at Gabe.

"Hi, honey," Windsor sings, and they share a big phony peck.

"Rick, how are ya, bud?" Gabe asks. He shakes Rick's hand but gives him no time to respond. "Marie, good to see you," he says to Mom, and they do a clumsy half shake, half hug. Gabe tips his chin around the room. "Kids, good to meet ya. Charles, good ol' Charlie." He reaches to tousle Charles's hair, but Charles ducks his hand. If Gabe notices, he doesn't show it. He doesn't even say hi to Kat, like he's wise enough not to.

"So how was the drive?" He goes to the fridge to get a drink, and the way he does it is like *Look at me, in my house, drinking my beer.*

"It was fine," Rick says. "No traffic."

"Oh yeah? That's good." He talks too loud and slurps too loud, leans on the counter with his hip.

"We went to the zoo. That little desert zoo" is Mom's contribution to this painful exchange.

"Yeah? The zoo?" The way Gabe talks, it's clear he's learned how to show interest when really he could give two farts.

"Oh!" Windsor pipes in. "I've always wanted to take the kids there. It's on my route." The conversation drops then like a hole in the floor. The silence is profound.

"Well, all right. You wanna talk or what?" Gabe suddenly blurts, as if the quiet is a personal insult.

"Yes, let's talk," Rick says, all business. "Kids, why don't you go and play outside?"

Outside, Kat flicks her hand and says, "Whatever," and stomps down the stairs. They know better than to follow her around. There's nowhere to play, really, so they just wander. Nobody's saying much, except Tiny, who blabs on and on because he doesn't know when to shut his hole. "I wonder what show they're watchin' in that house. Or that one? You think they're watchin' the same thing? What do you think it is? *Who's the Boss?* What time is it? I bet it's *Who's the Boss?*"

"Shut up," Charles says, so sharply that Tiny does.

Charles finds a stick and starts tapping things with it. Not hitting, not smacking, just *tap* mailbox, *tap* big stone, *tap* bumper on a truck. Last summer, last June, Charles tackled one of the trailer park kids and punched him, over and over, until the kid's face was bloody and some of his teeth had fallen out. It took three adults to pull Charles off. When he came home at the end of the weekend, Mom and Rick sat him down for a solemn talk, but he didn't even defend himself, didn't really say a word. Thing is, the kid had dropped a runt into a bucket of paint thinner. When he put the lid on and refused to take it off, Charles beat the shit out of him. Didn't matter. The puppy still died.

"Look," Bubbles says, because there's a hornet's nest in the park's only tree. They take turns trying to peg it with rocks.

When they get back to the trailer, the grown-ups are all standing on the porch and Kat's pulling open the door of the van.

"So?" Charles says to her. He's still holding that stick like it's the only thing he's got.

"So nothin'," she says back and yanks her overnight bag from the van.

"All right, kids. Let's go!" Mom calls, her voice cheery as though something's been resolved—which seems impossible because Gabe's still standing there, holding his beer. Why had they even come? Driven all the way out to Apple Valley, bothered with that miserable zoo? Obviously Rick hadn't seen anything damning, and what was he supposed to do? Ask? Rummage through drawers? Short any real evidence, the only thing to do was shake the guy's hand and go home. It's not like it's illegal to be an asshole.

The sad thing, though, the part that will stick with Nenny for years, is how different Kat and Charles are when Windsor comes to Kensington Drive. They seem to orbit her at a careful distance, at once drawn to her but wary of getting too close, like planets that circle lest they collide. Here, though, at Happy Trails, they've become toughened and hard-hearted and cruel. Windsor keeps choosing Gabe, over and over, for whatever reason, and it's a betrayal each and every time.

Kat and Windsor are still on the porch as they leave. Nenny watches them through the window of the van. Whenever people say how much she looks like Windsor, Kat wrinkles her nose and makes noises of disgust, but it can't be denied—same flaxen hair, same grey-green eyes. Both have their arms crossed and they're not saying much, they're not even looking at each other, really. Who knows how long they'll stay there, the thing between them a storm, Windsor on one step and Kat on the other, like a cloud casting a shadow on another cloud.

Matt Er Horn

A FEW days later Mom's shouting, "For Chrissake, Charles! That's enough!" because he's always dumping more sugar into his bowl—sugar on the Cocoa Puffs, sugar on the Trix, sugar on the Lucky Charms—when out of nowhere Tiny *leaps* out of his chair and starts shouting, *"We won! We won! We won!"* He's looping and whooping around the room, and they all look at one another like *What is going on?* Finally Mom crouches and catches him mid-lap. "What did we win, honey? What did we win?" Without answering, he breaks free and bolts upstairs and comes back with these box tops, there must be hundreds of box tops spilling from his hands. He's like a clown with all that bubbling, incomprehensible glee. Finally they manage to piece it together: if you collect a certain number of box tops, General Mills will send you and your family to Disneyland. Turns out, Tiny's good for something after all.

But when Rick gets home, he immediately starts reading the fine print. "Says here we've still got to pay a fee." And there's finer print too. General Mills will send you and your family of *four,* not four rug rats, two exhausted parents, and a snotty talk-back teen. Guess General Mills never got the memo. News flash: the nuclear family doesn't exist anymore. The nuclear family got nuked.

But who's listening to Rick? Fine print, shmine print. They've never—if you can believe it—been to Disneyland before. Dad took Nenny and the boys to Knott's Berry Farm after the divorce, but it is *not* the same. It's fine if you like stupid kid rides and jars of jam. Knott's is filled with old people who just love jars of jam. The only redeeming thing about it is this tilty room where water pours up instead of down, but still. It ain't Disneyland. Disneyland's right across the street, and if you think it doesn't hurt to be that close and not go in, you've got another think coming. It hurts you in the back of the jaw. Hurts you right in the teeth.

Point is: it'll be the best day ever! They're going to Disneyland! And *this?* This is what happiness feels like. Real happiness, real joy, is your brother waving a bunch of box tops around. It's your other brothers stomping on the couch, chanting, "Matt Er Horn! Matt Er Horn!" Not one but three glorious little words. It's your sister already squealing into the phone, and Mom without a worry in the world, playfully pulling Rick's arm. *Matt Er Horn! Matt Er Horn!* And Rick, though he's the most tightfisted son of a gun in the world, Rick just nodding and smiling a little bit, because it's already decided you'll go.

The Crappiest
Place on Earth

NENNY'S NOT positive, but she's pretty sure the definition of re-
bellion is wearing a Knott's Berry Farm T-shirt to Disneyland.
She imagines the horror on Mickey's face, those dark rumored
tunnels where surely they'll drag her the minute she arrives.
When they get there, though, nobody even notices—or if they
do notice, they don't care. Other things too: Mom gets all
caught up in the bank of gift shops at the entrance, then insists
they all stand in front of the castle for a family photo. They
have to wait for Tiny to quit being a jerk and making jerk faces,
and for all the other families to stop walking into the frame,
and it takes about ten years before they get to their first ride.
It's Alice in Wonderland, and for the record, it's super lame. In
fact, a lot of the rides are lame. It's like they're designed for children by children or something. And that's not all: Small World
gets stopped and everyone on it sternly warned because the kids
in front of them keep sticking their hands in the water, Space
Mountain is closed, Rick gets all weirdly enchanted by this
dumb movie in Tomorrowland where the narrator keeps saying
"In the future..." as if the future isn't right now, because it's all

shots of microwaves and cars and stuff that already exists. They break to get hot dogs, and there's this band singing on a stage, and when they sing "I Wanna Dance with Somebody"—which is Nenny's absolute favorite song of all time—she runs up to Mom and says, "Mom! Whitney Houston is here! She's singing on that little stage!" But before Mom can even open her mouth, Kat snorts and says, real loud, practically screams, "You idiot! That lady's white," and the people around them all start laughing and Nenny wants to die, she just wants to die right there, because she doesn't know what Whitney Houston looks like and that seems like the kind of thing you ought to know. Then, to top it off, the stupid lady at the hat shack spells out NANNY on her mouse ears, and Mom goes, "It's fine, it's fine," because there's about a billion kids waiting for their ears and you can tell Mom's tired and doesn't want to stand around anymore. Some kid gets diarrhea in the Tiki Room, like serious explosion, and it takes the staff about two hours before they realize it and open the doors. When they get outside, Charles yells, "More like the crappiest place on earth!" and that sets Rick off, who yanks him aside and spanks him, kinda hard. Charles starts crying, and Charles *never* cries. Kat is so over it by then she just keeps saying, "Oh my god. Oh my god." By the time they get to the Matterhorn ride in Fantasyland, no one's singing "Matt Er Horn" anymore. It's like they forgot they even had a chant. It's actually scary as hell, all those glowing red eyes, and when they get off, boom: Bubbles starts puking, really just puking all over the place. The guy who works the ride—his name tag says SVEN, but you can tell it's fake—he's nice about it and all, even keeps up his stupid Matterhorn accent, "Oh, nooh! Looks lyke ve've had un accident," but gives it up when Bubbles heaves again and this time ralphs on the guy's shoe.

In short? It kind of sucks. Disneyland kind of sucks.

Except, maybe, for this: there's supposed to be an evening fireworks show over Tom Sawyer Island, and they get there early and land a good spot. Mom'd wanted to go home when Bubbles got sick, but Rick said no way and reminded her of the fee. Bubbles seems fine now anyways, asleep in a ball on the grass. They're all sprawled on a little hill, and Mom's sitting by Rick, and when the fireworks start, she leans into him and he puts his arm around her. Nenny watches them out of the corner of her eye and realizes she's never really seen them like this before, affectionate and totally at ease. She can't decide if it's nice or strange, but when the fireworks start and everyone's face becomes beautifully lit, she realizes it's nice, all this, and not strange at all.

It's fleeting, though, the niceness. With all the dumb people, it takes like an hour just to get out of the stupid parking lot. Of course, the instant they hit the freeway, Bubbles pukes again, right there in the car.

December 9

AND THEN, the phone rings. It's December 9th, just a few ago-
nizing weeks until Christmas. Their wish lists are already taped
to the fridge. Bubbles wants an Erector set and a new belt. Kat
wants a dual cassette radio, which isn't cheap. Tiny wants the
Ghostbusters fire station, and Charles—big surprise—wants the
entire G.I. Joe Tiger Force Brigade. What Nenny wants is simple: she wants to lie, for hours, under the tree, with the quiet of
the lights dancing on the branches, her face round and bent in
a million bulbs, and for that to be the only feeling in the world.
Just the endless colors of Christmas nights. Mom can crawl under too, and maybe she laughs when the needles get caught in
her hair, or finds and holds Nenny's hand. Tiny will probably
see their legs poking out and get jealous—he can come if he
promises not to be dumb. Bubbles of course can come because
he's always easy and nice. Charles can come too if he lets his inside doors stay open and doesn't act mean. They all scooch their
bottoms so everyone can fit, even Kat, if she's in one of her new,
rare, singing moods. She just joined the choir at school and now
sometimes she sings, just for the heck of it, and even Nenny has

to admit it's pretty and unexpected, like smoothing crumpled tin. She can come if she sings "O Holy Night" in a nice way, a good way, a way that makes Mom cry but quietly, pretending like she isn't. Even Rick. Rick can come too. That's what Nenny wants, all seven of them, simple and unruffled and uncomplicated and unhurt, snuggling and giggling under the tree.

Of course, she can't write that. She writes "Happy Holidays Barbie" instead and knows that most wishes, anyways, don't come true.

—⁂—

December 9th. The phone rings. It's early morning, right before school, and everyone's in a panic to get things done—Tiny to find some pants, Bubbles to find his math book, Charles his brain. Kat's already left, because she gets a ride with Leah, her new choir friend. Rick calls from the top of the stairs, "Whoever's ready in five can come with me!" Of course they're scrambling because otherwise they'll have to walk. And sure, it's not ten feet of snow and below freezing in the San Bernardino Valley, but walking's walking and they'd rather get a ride.

And then the phone rings, and Nenny's closest to it so she picks it up.

"Hello?"

"Nenny. This is Keith. Can I speak with your mom?"

Keith is Kat and Charles's uncle, Windsor's brother. Nenny's never met him, only heard about him—he lives in Berkeley and works at a science lab, his wife does ballet. He seems nice enough, so Nenny says, "Sure," and calls upstairs. It doesn't occur to her why he might be calling so early, or why he's asking for Mom.

Something must occur to Mom, though, because she says, "Keith?" in a peculiar way, her chin tipped to the side, then says, "I'll take it in my room."

Nenny notices that she closes the door. In this house there are hardly ever phone calls behind closed doors.

—⚬—

December 9th. Phone rings. Bubbles is shouting, "Hurry up! Hurry up!" while books and rulers spill from his bag. His laces are untied, his zipper's down. Nenny picks up the phone. "Nenny? It's Keith." Mom takes the call in her room. Mom shuts the door.

—⚬—

It's 7:30 a.m. and the house is a shit show before school. Charles runs from room to room, looking for the cat, "Joe! Joey! Joe!"—why's he looking for the cat?—and Bubbles opens and closes books, searching for his homework, and Kat's shouting "See ya!" as she slams the front door, and Rick yells, "Three minutes!"

The phone rings, Nenny answers, Mom takes the call in her room, and Tiny shouts, "Oh no!" because he's clogged the toilet again so there's a scramble to find the plunger, and Charles finally has the cat but no shirt, and Bubbles says, "Put on a shirt, freak," and Charles says, testily, "Don't tell me what I am." Before long, but who knows how long, they're ready and waiting for Rick.

"Hey, what time is it?" someone says, because time got suddenly weird. They're all sitting on the stairs.

The door opens then, and Rick comes out onto the landing. There are so many moments in any given day, and on December the 9th there's got to be a moment, though hard to pinpoint, when Nenny realizes something is wrong.

"You guys go ahead and walk to school." Is this the moment? Sitting on the stairs?

"We'll be late," Nenny protests, looking up at him.

"I'll write a note." Is this it? Does Rick write notes?

But no. Here it is. Here's the moment right here: Nenny looks up and sees Mom, quickly passing behind the open bedroom door, and though her head's bent, and she's only visible for a flash, even from here Nenny can tell she's crying.

—⁓—

"Maybe he's in jail."

"What?"

"I said maybe he's in jail."

"Who? Keith?"

"No, Michael Jackson."

"Why would Keith be in jail?"

"I dunno. Maybe he killed someone."

"Yeah, right."

They're walking to school, the clouds above like a sheet laid across the sky. Nenny's got Rick's note tucked in her pocket. It says, "Wallace/Sutter children late. Please excuse."

"Keith is not in jail," Charles says, with such authority that they believe him, though how could he know? He walks with his chin down, hands clutching his backpack straps. They're not in a hurry by any means, but there's something furrowed and determined about him, moving forward like a plow.

"Maybe someone died?" Bubbles says gently.

"Who?"

"Your Gramma Sadie, maybe?"

And Charles looks at him then with something indiscernible on his face, like trying to solve a puzzle when you haven't got any clues. They're all quiet for a moment because that's a thing, that's a possibility, for grandmas to die.

They move through the crackle of dead leaves. Other things occur to Nenny because other things always do: Keith has a rare form of cancer, his wife is being held for ransom, he was at the lab and acid splashed in his face, they lost all their money in a crazy bet and now they've got nowhere to live.

"Maybe their house burnt down," she says and feels it as the worst possible thing, for their house to burn down.

"I doubt it," Charles says, but he doesn't look at her. He walks along, steadily, shoving his feet through leaves.

—∞—

When they get to school, the secretary takes the note and says, "Hm," like it's forged or suspect, but gives them each a pass.

—∞—

December 9, 1988: Enter your classroom with the secretary's note. Hand it to Sister Timothy, who scowls. Go to your desk. Put your backpack at your feet. Arithmetic. You're terrible at math. Your homework looks like a war zone. Pay whatever attention you can. Next, history. Egyptians preserved in elaborate tombs. Notice that Matty Souza is smiling in his seat. Smiling at you? Forget that someone might have died. See Charles on the way to lunch, his slouch, his vacant eyes. Remember again. Spend the rest of the day in a liquid, faltering haze.

—∞—

When they get home, Mom and Rick are both there. Something is palpably wrong. Kat walks in, and whatever is in the room is thick, a terrible fog.

"What the hell is going on?"

—∞—

December 9, 1988. What the hell is going on?

—∞—

Mom takes Nenny and Tiny and Bubbles to Uncle Max's house because Dad is still at work. They don't ask questions, just pile into the car because Mom says to. Usually when Mom drives she'll put on Queen's *Greatest Hits* and everyone will sing along, but they know it's not that kind of drive.

Out of nowhere, Tiny says, "I'm scared." Everyone hears it, though it's nearly a whisper. Outside, the last of the orange groves slides past as they drive into a low canyon where the gravel company is, the huge craters of their operations like wounds in the sand.

—∞—

Tiny says, "I'm scared," but what's there to be scared of? They're just driving with Mom. Except there's no Queen and outside the ground has been blasted to bits, earth exploded just to reach more earth, and Mom blinks then, long and slow, and looks at Tiny in the rearview, then at Bubbles, then over at Nenny, that look, how slow.

—⦿—

Uncle Max is standing at the kitchen sink with a glass of wine at four in the afternoon. Chester is nowhere around, though Nuisance is, curled under a chair. They come in through the back door, and Uncle Max and Mom look at each other, how adults share looks, and he points to the living room, and Mom takes them there and closes the door.

—⦿—

The living room is carved from another era. Carpet as thick and white as a slain bear's fur, furniture all dark and low and teak, the couch like a big hand.

—⦿—

Mom closes the door and helps them off with their coats. Quietly, Tiny begins to cry. Who knows why, but everyone knows why— the phone had rung, Uncle Keith, no Queen. Mom pulls her sleeve over her palm and wipes his face, and then she's crying too. They sit on the couch that's like a big hand and Mom tells them what they've been waiting to be told but could never have seen coming.

"Windsor was killed."

Nenny was right. There was an awful thing.

This is it. This is the awful thing.

—⁓—

This is a true and terrible story. As with all things terrible and true, the details do not emerge at once, but leak slowly and painfully out over the course of many years.

Two days earlier, police found Windsor's body in the back of her delivery van. She was naked, hog-tied, and had been shot through the back of her head. Authorities guessed that some addicts had seen a van marked MEDICAL SUPPLY, assumed there were drugs on board, and somehow coerced Windsor—who was always, Rick said, picking up hitchhikers and hippie kids—into giving them a ride. Presumably when they discovered their mistake—that "supply" was not pharmaceutical, but walkers and ACE wraps and bedpans—they panicked and killed her. Whoever they were, they were never caught.

The strange thing—the thing that takes this from terrible to confusing and bizarre—is that a week later, thirty miles away, on a bench at a bus shelter in Barstow, the police found Windsor's clothes in a neat pile, as if they'd been folded with the tenderest of care.

—⁓—

When they get home from Max's late that night, Charles is playing Super Mario in the den downstairs. They stand in the doorway because it's clear he doesn't want to talk, and anyway what would they say? *Sorry about your mom. You can share ours now?* They stand quietly and watch him while he lets himself be watched. Slowly the boys move into the room and stand behind him, then scoot forward and sit down, and without a word he hands them each a controller and, sound off, they play.

Upstairs, Kat is on her bed, crying. She's on her back with her arms over her face, and when Nenny comes in, she looks up, her face streaked with tears.

"Did I hug her?" she says through hiccupped breaths.

Nenny moves close because she's not sure she's heard right.

"Did I hug her? Last time she was here? Did I hug her good-bye?"

Most people will tell you that lying is wrong, that lying is a sin. But some lies need to be told, some lies mean everything—and if anyone tells you they don't, then let anyone be damned.

"Yes, you did. I saw you," Nenny says and puts her hand on Kat's back. "I was standing on the landing and you did."

But of course, Nenny has no idea.

FEAR #1: DISAPPEARED

MOM, FOR whatever reason, doesn't come home.

They never see her again.

House Two:
Citrus Grove

Decisions

JANUARY HITS hard and heavy as a fist. It's colder, it seems, than it's ever been. Mornings, frost spreads like fingers across panes of glass, and small puddles are capped with thin sheets of ice. Smudge pots smolder in the orange groves, which hasn't happened, apparently, for years.

At Kensington, decisions have been made: Nenny and the boys will move in with Dad, just for a little while, just until things "settle down." As if settling down's what you do when someone's been killed. The kids aren't consulted on the matter—children never are. Adults will ask you what flavor ice cream you want, what show you want to watch, if you want your hair down or in braids, but they won't consult you on the most basic questions of where and how you want to live.

Like this: they'd buried Windsor the week after Christmas, and Nenny and the boys did not go. No one asked them if they cared to. It was assumed that because Windsor was not their mother, that because they'd only met her a handful of times, they would not be affected by her death, as if being in the same family tree is the only way to feel if someone's died. If there was a dusty church, they did not see it. If there was a moving eulogy, they had no idea. If Gabe came in drunk and Gramma Sadie collapsed on the floor and wailed because someone, some monster, had stolen her daughter's life, there was no way for them to know. When Kat and Charles came home from the funeral and went silently into their separate rooms, Nenny and the boys were left to imagine what happened, which everyone knows only makes things worse.

Now a suitcase yawns open on the bed like a howling mouth, and Nenny has to pack for a weekend with no end. A suitcase and an interminable weekend and questions about what this means are all vast, gaping holes—no matter how hard you try, they cannot be filled.

"Don't worry, honey," Mom says later, somehow guessing at Nenny's true thoughts: *What happens now? What about Charles and Kat?* "You'll see each other on weekends and at school."

As if that's enough, as if that could ever be enough.

Citrus Grove

CITRUS GROVE apartment complex isn't exactly a crap hole, but it's far from luxurious. All the apartment doors are painted red, as if this eccentric splash of color could compensate for termites gnawing the walls or a swimming pool that's never cleaned. The inhabitants are people like Dad, regular folks, teachers and public service workers and electricians, single moms and single dads and young families struggling to grab ahold of some kind of one-income respect, people too busy or bothered to swim. The superintendent's name is Chuck Baldy, a name that describes better than any adjectives can.

Dad lives in 3B, a two-bedroom on the second floor that he struggles to keep tidy. Shelves bow heavy with the weight of his movies and books, his "memorabilia" spread around like shrapnel. He's cleaned things up for the big change: where once there were button-downs slung like corpses over chairs, there's now a laundry basket by the couch where errant socks and undershirts can rest in peace. He's done the dishes, all of them, cleaned the clutter off the counters, and the paper-grading table has been cleared off and restored to its original purpose as a place to eat.

He answers the door nervously when they knock, as if unsure how to proceed in his own apartment, with his own kids.

"They're all set," Mom says, indicating their bags. "Play clothes, uniforms..."

Dad nods vigorously, which is a weird way to nod given the circumstances. Suddenly, Tiny bursts into tears.

"Oh, sugar," Mom sighs. She crouches and pulls him close. "You're okay."

"C'mon, now," Dad says weakly. "You're gonna have fun here."

And Nenny thinks, *He's six, he's not stupid.* This is about being marooned—it's not about fun. Every night for the past week, Kat has lain in her bed across from Nenny, a pillow pulled over her face, and cried. Nenny is nine years old. Everything she's ever learned about anything (state capitals; planets; the difference between verbs and nouns; war exists and in war everyone kills everyone, stupid) is wholly inadequate and offers zero groundwork for what has come and for what lies ahead. With a shotgun and a coil of rope, someone has ripped to shreds the cloak between the world that is and the world that isn't, and exposed not imagined fears—earthquakes and thieves and the ghosts of the Vietcong—but instead the cold, naked truth: the world is a terrible, ugly place, and here we are in it.

"Tell you what," Dad says, putting his hand on Tiny's shoulder. "I'll call the super and see about cleaning the pool."

By the Pool

Boots is the kind of person you can talk with about anything. You don't have to pretend you're feeling something you aren't, or aren't feeling something you are. Boots knows something of the world because her grandfather shot himself, late last year. He'd been diagnosed with cancer and couldn't bear to suffer what was to come. Her aunt found him on the porch.

"Oh my god," Nenny says when Boots tells her. "What was ... I mean, what—"

"His brains?" Boots finishes her thought. "His brains were everywhere. They had to build a new porch."

The girls are sitting by the pool. Chuck Baldy, the superintendent, told Dad he'd fix it up two weeks ago, but it's doubtful that will happen by summer. It's still a decrepit swamp. Yellow algae floats faintly on the surface of the water. They swirl it back and forth with sticks.

"What'd she do?"

"Who?"

"Your aunt, when she found him."

"Oh. My mom said she got sick, then called the police."

"Got sick?"

"Threw up."

"Oh." It's hard not to imagine the scene: an old man toppled over in a lawn chair, his legs frozen midair, blood and goo and brains, his daughter puking her guts out. Nenny thinks of the officer who found Windsor. He probably didn't throw up because cops are used to that sort of thing. But then again, maybe he did.

"What about your grandma? Is she, like, okay?"

"Okay?" Boots stops to think, her swirling stick paused. "She's not as fun anymore."

Nenny doesn't need her to explain. Here's the thing that sets Boots apart from everyone, everywhere: other people, grownups, they lie straight to your face, pat your arm and say "It'll be okay." But not Boots. Boots's dad left Boots and her mom when she was just four years old, so she knows a thing or two about a thing or two and does not beat around the bush and would never lie.

"It's stupid," Boots says after a pause.

"What's stupid?"

"When someone dies."

"Yeah," Nenny says, and swirls her stick some more. Above, the awful stillness of a winter sky.

What Nuns Should Do

THE FIRST day back at school and everyone stares. Nenny and the boys have taken two weeks off to move and to readjust, and in that time the news of their tragedy has spread like a vapor through every classroom, down every hall. When Dad drops them off, a visible flutter moves through the crowd of students playing on the asphalt before the bell. They all turn and stare like something's fallen. Finally, Sister Renata, Tiny's nun, blows her whistle to put an end to whatever this is and to signal the start of class. Lines begin to form. Nenny watches as Renata kneels before Tiny and puts her hand on his shoulder and says something that Nenny can't hear, but it must be something comforting and sweet, because that's what nuns should do.

Should do, but often don't. Sister Timothy starts class without a word, just taps her yardstick on the desk and says, "Geography, please." Everyone takes their homework from their desks, except Nenny, who's been led to believe she's been excused, in a note from Mother Superior herself: "My deepest condolences to your family. As far as work the children have missed, be assured they are excused." But Sister Timothy must not have seen the note.

"Nenny, your homework, please." She hasn't even finished flipping through the stack, and it's clear she's just illustrating some point.

"I don't have it," Nenny says.

"You'll have one week to catch up." She glances at Nenny over the ridge of her spectacles, as if to be sure Nenny's heard.

The day goes on like this. Nenny gets called on for questions she couldn't possibly know the answers to, is beckoned to the board to take notes, is told over and over to read certain passages aloud. It doesn't take long before the day's message is clear, to everyone: you will not get any soothing or comfort here, just a solid, first-class education.

But when the final bell rings, Sister says, "Nenny, you'll stay." Everyone lingers a minute to stare before they trickle out the door.

"I hear there's been a death in your family," Sister says from behind her desk.

"Yes, ma'am." So she did get the note.

"Charles's mother?"

"Yes."

"I imagine that's not been easy." But, strangely, she says it in a way that demonstrates she's never imagined anything at all.

Nenny nods. It's clear they are not bonding—you can't bond with a piece of steel. Still, Nenny had not expected any special treatment, and certainly not this: Sister Timothy acknowledging, however distantly, that this whole thing has been hard. If charity is a branch, a line of salvation and mercy that we extend to one another in our darkest hours, then that might be what this is. It's not soothing, and it's not comfort, but in her own bizarre, chiseled way, Sister Timothy is perhaps extending the thinnest branch. It's enough to make Nenny begin to cry.

"Now, now," Sister says as Nenny sniffles. "Let's keep things in perspective. She wasn't your mother, after all."

And there goes the branch.

Night

BEFORE THEY moved in, Dad bought Nenny a bed and cleared the junk out of his office so she could have her own room. It's darker than her room at Mom's. At Mom's there's a window overlooking the street, but this room is like a vault. It faces the alley and the back of the Christian radio station. There's a mural of an angel there, sort of flying or leaning forward, holding a microphone instead of a trumpet. The angel doesn't really have a face, just the shadowed suggestions of one.

The boys sleep in Dad's room, and Dad sleeps on the couch. It doesn't even fold out, and when he wakes in the morning his face looks flattened and mowed, but he doesn't complain. At breakfast he struggles to stay awake, yawning and rubbing his eyes, while other times he stands with one hand on the counter and the other on his back, wearing a look of having been stabbed. He doesn't say anything (*The couch sucks. You kids take up too much space*), so Nenny doesn't either (*The bed is lumpy. I don't want to sleep in this dark room*). All those things Rick used to say about sacrifice are finally sinking in. She hangs a poster of the New Kids above her bed and pretends this is working, pretends this is home.

But then night comes. Night arrives as a soundless bully, shoving and charging and slamming into the room. To the left side Nenny rolls but does not sleep, and to the right side she rolls but does not sleep, and straight above is the ceiling light like a watchful eye. She misses Mom. She longs for Mom like being torn apart, a dull ache of longing like a ribbon unspooling from the center of her chest. Kensington is only a few miles from here but seems forever away. She traces the route in her mind—up Brookside to Citrus to Wabash, past the YMCA and the high school, past the 7-Eleven and the orange groves—and hates distances, hates roads, wishes hungrily and desperately and feverishly that she was in her other house, asleep or not, it doesn't matter, only that Mom is just down the hall. Nenny loves Dad, but Dad is not enough.

She hears his snores coming down the hall and thinks, *How can anyone sleep with night like this, when someone's been killed?* Two men, three men—however many men—how can you sleep when they haven't been caught? Night comes and with it filthy blue jeans and calloused hands, breath like a wet ashtray and hair that hasn't been washed, yellow and crooked and horrible teeth, killer teeth, men stomping their boots and walking away, stopping however briefly to fold a dead woman's clothes.

Return

It's the Friday of their first weekend back at Mom's. Nenny is nervous and doesn't know why—but of course she knows why. She spends the school day trying to concentrate, but her mind keeps wandering off. A deep hungry need surges through her, a need that would embarrass her if spoken out loud. She pictures entering the house on Kensington Drive, the smell of spaghetti and meatballs, everything as it was a week ago—the beanbag chair still in the den, the seascape painting still on the wall— pictures what it will be like when Mom rounds the corner when Nenny and the boys come in. Nenny should be practicing her spelling and doing math, but instead she's imagining running through the hall and leaping into Mom's open arms, and Mom dropping to one knee to catch her, to hold her close, to stroke her hair. *Nenny, I've missed you so much! I hate it when you're not here!*

None of that happens. Dad picks them up from school and this time walks them to the door. Bubbles knocks formally instead of walking in, which is weird because a week ago this was their primary home. Rick answers the door and his face registers surprise to see Dad standing there, holding Tiny's

Scooby-Doo suitcase. When Rick reaches out for a handshake, Dad takes his hand sort of limply, as if he doesn't quite remember what purpose a handshake serves. The two men don't talk much, and after a minute Dad just says, "Well, okay," and walks back to the car. Nenny and the boys won't see him again until Monday. It's hard to fathom how he survives on his own.

Nenny's need for Mom is so great she's almost shivering. She wants to run to Mom like a hungry wolf, a week's worth of longing catapulting through her blood—but the need is quickly compacted and compressed, because when Mom rounds the corner from the kitchen, she looks not like she wants to be leapt upon or clung to or hugged but rather as though some part of her, something essential, has been erased.

"Hi, guys," she says, toweling her hands. She hugs each of them distractedly, shoulder squeezing and quick, the kind of hug a camp counselor might give. "Put your things away and wash up. Dinner will be ready soon." Nenny and the boys wait as if for something else, but she's already back at the stove. Kat and Charles are not around.

Nenny feels crazed. What is happening? Rick hardly greeted them, is already in the den watching the news. Neither has asked how their week was, how they're doing, what life is like at Dad's, if they want to move back. They're acting as if Nenny and the boys are returning from a quick jaunt around the block. She looks at Bubbles for confirmation, to see if he feels it too, but he refuses to meet her gaze. Eyes fixed down, he trudges up the stairs. Even Tiny is quiet. So it's clear: everything has changed. They are now visitors here.

Kat is on her bed when Nenny comes in, writing in a notebook on a pillow spread across her knees. Her hand moves steadily, as though she writes all the time, which she doesn't.

Nenny sets her backpack on the floor, and Kat keeps working—not rudely, just focused. It's so quiet she can hear Kat's pen scratching across the page.

Finally, Kat looks up. "Hi," she says. She's wearing a grey sweatshirt and jeans, no makeup or earrings, and looks at Nenny with a steady, not-bitchy gaze. "Hi," Nenny says meekly, then searches for something else to say. She doesn't know what to do, so she leaves for the bathroom and closes the door. Nenny feels misplaced and unwanted, or worse than unwanted: unseen. Mom always notices if something is wrong with Nenny—and now that's not even true. Something shifts inside her, and it's like a knob being turned, but she can't break down because that wouldn't be fair. Like Sister Timothy said, it wasn't her mom who died. Turning on the faucet, Nenny scoops handfuls of water and brings them to her cheeks, splashing her face over and over so she will not cry.

Charles is standing in the hallway when she opens the door. Nenny starts; she had no idea he was there.

"Took you long enough," he says, shoving off from the wall. "You got the squirts or something?" He says it as an accusation, something to embarrass her, and it works. It's only been a week since she last saw him—he and Kat are still out of school—but he looks as if he hasn't washed or slept in months. His hair is slick with grease and there are dark circles under his eyes, purple like bruises.

"Move. I gotta pee." She steps aside, and he pushes past her, closing the door. In the bedroom, Kat's still writing on her bed, this time with headphones on. She doesn't seem to notice Nenny coming in. Nenny takes out a book and tries to read, but the lack of chaos and noise is too foreign and isolating. She wants so much to go home, to be home, but she doesn't know where home is anymore, if it even exists.

A Boy

IF YOU want to expose and mangle a boy's humanity, wrench his mother from him at an early age. Take her, and watch the light drain from his face. Watch his skin pale and his eyes darken, his shoulders hunch like a creature curling so far into itself that it finally disappears.

In the hallways at school, across the cafeteria during lunch, Nenny watches Charles with the gaze of a cautious observer. Other boys slam the trash can lid and gurgle their milk, make faces and rude gestures behind the nuns' backs, but Charles sits among them like a ghost. On weekends he plays video games for hours on end, eats without enthusiasm, and mostly just shuts himself in his room.

One Thursday, a few weeks after they've been back at school, Donnie Harlem slinks up to Charles from across the lunchroom. Donnie Harlem is puny and has deeply glazed eyes. His mother lives in Egypt and his father's seldom around, and he lives with his aunt and uncle in an apartment behind the school. Everyone knows all this, in the way that everyone knows everything.

"Hey, Charles," he coos, like they're old chums, old pals.

Charles is twice as tall as Donnie, but Donnie leans in anyway, both hands on the wobbly table.

Charles regards Donnie with tepid disdain, like considering an insect he can't be bothered to squish. With his sandwich near his mouth, he looks at Donnie, then takes a bite.

Donnie leans in closer and glances around to see who's watching. People are. Donnie's the kind of kid who people watch, hoping he doesn't watch back. The clatter of the lunchroom is nearly deafening, but a building scene is a building scene, and Donnie Harlem's always building a scene.

He grabs a Cheeto off Charles's plate and pops it into his mouth. Charles watches him chew.

"So," Donnie says, and what happens next is horrifying because it is entirely true. He leans in again and without a flinch looks right into Charles's eyes. "I heard your mom got her brains blown out."

Take a boy, any boy, and move his mother to Egypt. Give his dad a drug problem, and make sure he's not around. Throw a drunk, violent uncle into the mix, and see where the boy ends up. Put him in a room with an audience, face-to-face with another defeated, windblown boy, and see what happens. You'd be surprised what happens.

Nothing, really. The Charles of a month ago would've been blind with rage, would've pummeled Donnie until his face bled, as he did the boy at Happy Trails Park. But this Charles is new. This Charles has no need to defend what is sacred, because nothing is anymore.

He doesn't say anything. Donnie waits, grinning, because he's the kind of kid who wants this, wants anything, even if it's getting punched in the face. But Charles just lays his sandwich on the tray, picks it up, and walks away.

Any Boy

SEVEN YEARS later, Donnie Harlem suffers a heroin overdose in his aunt's garage. He is sixteen years old.

Take a boy, any boy.

Undone

BUBBLES BEGINS to take things apart. Normally he's putting them together, building Lego complexes and Erector set towers but now, if it can be undone, he undoes it. Radios, walkie-talkies, a tiny TV, whatever small appliance Dad won't notice is missing. He finds a square of cardboard and lays it on the deck, duct-tapes the corners down, and with a pair of pliers and a screwdriver the size of his thumb, he dismantles each device piece by piece by piece. Gears and knobs and coils and springs are arranged into meticulous, neat rows, Bubbles with his legs tucked beneath him, crouched concentrated and low, not saying a word, not saying anything at all, while the sun rises and falls behind the crow-crowded trees. Soon there's nothing left to deconstruct, and when that happens, he uses his measly allowance to buy gadgets at the Goodwill down the street—where the toys reek of rotten milk and the clerks have tired eyes—wears a camping headlamp in the middle of the day, takes Polaroid snapshots of the arranged parts because he read somewhere that's what mechanics do. In any other home, this kind of behavior would swell the curtains with a hopeful pride—"Your brother's going to be an engineer!"—but they don't have curtains in the apartment; they only have blinds.

Tiny, on the other hand, is mostly the same—totally annoying and always blabbing on and on. Manny Hernandez stepped on a bee and his foot "swoled to the size of a loaf," but when they took him to the hospital, the doctor said it wasn't a bee it was a "scorpsion" because its tail was still inside—even though every moron knows scorpions don't live around here. He sawded on a show that kangaroos are reladed to T. rex, which is how come their arms is like this, he says, and holds them crooked in front of his chest. There's one point five twillion stars in the sky, hamsters eat their young because they confuse them for pellets, you should always keep a first-aid kit in the car because one time Manny Hernandez's dad reached between the seats and there was a piece of glass there and he cutted his finger real bad (and one starts to wonder, does Manny Hernandez even exist?)—on and on and on, his jabbering, blabbering world made of half-dumb facts and half-imagined scenarios and half lies, which is a lot of halves but you get the point: Tiny won't shut up.

Until he does. Nights, the apartment is dark and still, the only sound Dad's deep snores traveling in syncopated bursts down the hall like echoes of some barge. Nenny lies awake and listens, pictures Dad's tongue clapping against the roof of his mouth, thinks of night, thinks of dawn, misses Mom terribly, thinks of Mom's hands, Mom's ears, the loneliness so fierce it's like a hole carved in the middle of her, a hole carved right into her chest. She rolls onto her side and is seized by a thought that's like being shook awake—which is that if she misses Mom this much and she's just across town, what must Charles and Kat feel?—when, from her bed, she sees Tiny appear at his door. He stands there in his Star Wars pajamas, not looking sleepy, not looking lost, just looking, for what it's worth, like a little boy. Moonlight pours through the window, lighting his face. Sometimes, Tiny goes quiet in the middle of the night, stands looking out the window before wandering down the hall, and in the morning is pressed sleeping against Dad on the couch, his thumb in his mouth, his legs flopped sloppily over Dad's legs. It's not a very big couch.

Roster

By THIRD grade, not everyone has suffered a loss—but many have. Nenny surveys the room.

Michael Barber: Michael's the kind of kid you feel sorry for without really knowing why. Pale white skin, teeth too crowded in his mouth. You could sort of see no one noticing if he got lost in a crowd.
Losses: His uncle, last spring. He was out of school for three days, and when he returned, he looked terrible. The bell had hardly rung when he took the bathroom pass and disappeared for twenty minutes. When he came back, it was clear he'd been crying, and it was sad, it really was, but it was hard not to be distracted by all the snot trailing out his nose.

Jessica Hall: Bright red hair and freckles, as though instead of being born she'd simply fallen from the sun. Jessica Hall wears sunglasses even on rainy days, and they look absurd on her freckled and sun-drenched face. It looks as though someone took an ax to her hairline, the burnt umber of her tender scalp. Everything about her is seared.

Losses: Her dog, Rosco, at the beginning of the year. She didn't seem too torn up about it, though.

Katie Marion: Everybody loves Katie Marion, just *loves* her, and what's not to love? Her with her stupid cheeks like polished apples and hair like a brushed doll's. She's got three sisters and they're all alike: angels that the teachers fawn over for their talents and their manners and their perfect, perfect grades. Katie Marion knows the answers to all the questions, she always says her prayers, she shares everything she's got, pretzels and Cheez-Its and stickers from a pack, and when they do the Pledge of Allegiance, she stands so perfectly erect, beaming and emotive and proud, that it seems like she actually *does* pledge allegiance. Katie Marion does not go through the motions. Katie Marion *is* the motions. She's everything.

Losses: Who knows? Who cares?

Jill McKenzie: Nenny and Jill used to be best friends, two years ago in first grade, but then Jill got commercial famous and couldn't be bothered with Nenny anymore. Commercial famous was a Ford print ad, where you couldn't really even see Jill's face, and a commercial on TV about juice. (The commercial was stupid and the juice wasn't very good.) It's not the fame that bothered Nenny; it's what Jill did with it. She came over to play once and looked at Nenny's dolls like they were dirty, and then threw up her milk and wanted to go home. One time Nenny saw her in the parking lot of Ralphs and Jill didn't even get out of the car, just rolled the window down to say hi. That was the beginning of the end. Nenny doesn't care, though. Now she's got Boots, who likes to take walks and will talk about whatever and isn't a snob in any way.

Losses: An older brother, who died in a terrible crash. He was really drunk when it happened. Not many people know all this, but Nenny does because Jill used to be her best friend.

Used to be.

Jackie Monroe: Jackie Monroe is weird. Like, really weird. She's always bringing random bunches of things to school, as if grouped together they make sense: a sewing bobbin with three hairpins; two bookmarks wrapped in newspaper; a broken charm bracelet and a photo of some-one on skis. At lunch she sits in the middle of the com-motion, humming and sipping soup. She's the only kid at Sacred Heart who brings soup.

Losses: Probably a lot, when her home planet was de-stroyed.

Franky O'Shea: In the first grade, Franky's mother—who at the time was a secretary at school—was arrested and sent to jail for assaulting a police officer. She'd been at an anti-abortion rally and become enraged and ended up punching a cop. It's hard to imagine: Ms. O'Shea (there was no mister, other than her sons), thin and lithe and with wispy red hair, hauling back and slugging some guy in the face. And then she was gone and the rumor spread and they hired a new secretary and then it was the end of the year. In September everyone watched Franky for some sign of change—his mother was still in jail, after all—but he just smiled and ran around with the other boys, red from the summer months. You could tell he was kind of faking it, though, all that exuberance, all that joy.

Losses: His mother, for a maximum of 3 years and a $10,000 fine.

Melissa Ryder: Melissa's father owns a yacht, Melissa says. She'll have her birthday party on it in the spring, she says. Everyone's invited, Melissa says. Her father owns a yacht, they vacation in Spain, they've got a pool like the kind in the Olympics—Melissa says, Melissa says, Melissa says. But when her mother comes to pick her up, every day after school, in a beat-up old van like a wad of crushed paper, like a turd, it's clear there's no truth in what Melissa says. Still, "You're all invited," she says, always says.

Losses: Don't believe anything Melissa says.

Steve Smoot: He'll eat pieces of paper, small ones, but only if they've got drawings of food on them. Jill draws a tiny apple, Steve Smoot wolfs it down. Michael draws a banana (or something like it), Steve Smoot wolfs it down. It's his party trick, except they're not at a party; they're at school.

Losses: He lives with his grandma and eats paper. You do the math.

Matty Souza: However unuttered, everyone agrees that whatever it is, whatever Matty's got, it's electrifying and rare. Everything he does is incredible, and not just the way he rolls his pants. The tiny air guitar he plays when he lip-syncs "La Bamba." The way he undoes an orange, aiming for an endless, unbroken peel; the way he seldom succeeds. His skin is buttered toast. His hair is raked with gold. The boys treat him as the ringleader of their awkward, bumbling gang, circling him like loyal dogs, and there's Matty, glancing around and blinking as if only now remembering they're there. Or on Valentine's Day each year, as his desk becomes piled with notes and candy and gifts, Matty regards his treasures as one might regard a strange light moving in the sky—with some confusion and some curiosity and perhaps, even, some fear. It isn't that he's dumb (Or who knows? Maybe he is.); it's that their unflinching, constant adoration completely eludes him. To be sure, that only increases the appeal: wherever he is in his gold-addled brain, he is there completely alone, a prince on a planet far, far away.

How disastrously easy it is to love someone who has no idea that he is loved.

Losses: (Oh, but his eyes! You should see his eyes!)

Michelle Wynne: Spend your whole life trying to understand a girl like Michelle Wynne—good luck with that. She's the only girl in the entire third grade who's allowed to wear makeup. Well, "allowed." Thick liner rims her eyes, and her lips glisten with pink gloss that she spends the day applying again and again. Mother Superior's talked to her about it a number of times, sent so many notes home that the notes begin to write themselves.

"Mr. and Mrs. Wynne, Please keep in mind the dress code when you send Michelle to school. Makeup is strictly prohibited." Or "Mr. and Mrs. Wynne, We are happy to have Michelle here, but she must comply with our rules."

Or "Mr. and Mrs. Wynne, Please." Sending letters home
really means no more than walking them across the street,
where the Wynnes live in a tangle of run-down duplexes.
It's the kind of place you can tell used to be cute, scalloped
edges on the buildings and a bird fountain in the courtyard. But the building's all faded now, broken screen doors
and dead grass and chipped paint. No water or birds in
the fountain anymore. Michelle Wynne doesn't pay tuition
at Sacred Heart. If you saw her mother and father, you
might be able to guess why, but no one's ever seen them
so then you knew why. Michelle is Sacred Heart's charity
case, and everyone is aware of this so they take pains not to
treat her any different—but you know how charity cases
are. There's a force field around them like a wall of snow.

Take, for example, this: Last year, for the Halloween fair,
Michelle came dressed in a tube top and a tiny skirt. Nenny
was (cleverly) a half boy, half girl; Franky was Peter Pan;
Matty Souza was it doesn't matter, he was Matty Souza;
and so on. But Michelle had on this tiny skirt, just a little afterthought of a thing, and with Magic Marker had
scribbled all over it: "Two-for-one special" and "Want to
spend some time?" She sat on a bench near the girls' bathroom, snapping her gum and bouncing her crossed legs,
her skinny, freckled little legs, hands on the bench, survey-
ing the crowd. Everyone knows a girl with charcoal eyes, a
girl whose parents never leave the house. Everyone knows,
but at the same time—second grade, bench outside the
bathroom—no one, not Nenny or Katie or Yvonne or any
of them, knew anything about anything yet.

"Michelle, what are you supposed to be?"

"I'm a bachelor's wife," she said. "It's the oldest profession in the world." She didn't even look at them, just looked out at the crowd, and no one had any idea what she was talking about. Mother Superior must've known, though, because at some point she came storming across the yard.

"Home, *now*." Her face was charred concrete, her hand shaking angrily as she pointed across the street. And you know Michelle: she just shrugged and got up off that bench and walked home, turning once to give a little toodle-loo wave.

Please, Mr. and Mrs. Wynne. Please.

Losses: Next year, her father, of a drug overdose. Charcoal eyes, beginning of the fourth grade.

New Nun

At the beginning of February, out of nowhere, Sister Timothy is sent to live in Holland—the children there must need a furious, boring dictator—and a new nun arrives. Her name is Mary. With a name like Mary you half expect a Maria type, with a voice like an angel singing, but Mary has yellowish teeth and grey hair poking from under her habit, deep wrinkles around her warm eyes, and a walk like an injured man's. First thing she says is "Oh no, this will never do" and makes them rearrange their desks into a circle. Then she says to José, "My dear, would you please open the blinds?" The sudden winter light is shocking, and the children all blink like moles as it spills into the room. Sister Timothy kept the blinds closed. She said things like "You will speak when spoken to" and "An idle mind is the devil's playground." She'd clap her hands to wake them, in a ruthless, unforgiving way, or rap her yardstick on their desks—*thwap*—to drive home her points. She never smiled and often shone with spiteful sweat.

Sister Mary is *not* Sister Timothy. This afternoon, after the students have gone home, she's going to take down all the bloody, sorrowful pictures of Jesus and replace them with the other Jesus, the one who sits in a field of eternal spring, smiling at a crowd of cheerfully dressed children and bright white sheep.

Right now she says, "You don't have music hour?" and everyone shakes their heads. As if it's the most incredible thing she's ever heard, she asks again. "Sister Timothy didn't teach music?"

No. Sister Timothy most definitely did not teach music. Mary gazes at them for a moment as if she's landed on an alien planet, where no one plays music and all Jesus does all day is cry.

"Well, all right," she sighs. "That's an easy enough problem to fix."

By the Pool

"WE GOT a new nun."

"You got a new nun? *I* want a new nun." And who knows what Boots even means by that, but they both laugh anyways.

"What's she like?"

Nenny shrugs. "She seems nice."

"That's good. The other one..."

"Sister Timothy."

"Yeah, her. She seemed like a bitch."

"Boots!"

"What? You know it's true."

"You can't call a nun a bitch."

"Why not?"

Good point.

"She wants us to learn the recorder," Nenny says.

"The what?"

"It's like a flute."

"That's cool. My uncle plays the flute." Boots throws a pebble and it plunks into the murky water.

Mr. Baldy comes out of his apartment then. "Hey, now! No messing with the pool!" he calls.

"Okay, Mr. Baldy!" Boots calls back.

This happens at least once a week, Mr. Baldy emerging from his apartment and calling, "Hey, now! No messing with the pool!" and Boots calling back, "Okay!" It's never an unfriendly exchange, and he seems nice enough. He seems like the kind of guy who would ask you how's school or what're you girls up to today—but maybe like he always forgets, like he's got other things on his mind.

—m—

Later, when Nenny hands Dad the information sheet about the recorder, he says, "Fifteen bucks? For a plastic flute?"

Nenny shrugs. "She says we need it."

"You need it? Flutes teach history now?" But he writes out a check anyways. On the little memo line, next to his signature, he writes "recorder," then scratches it out and writes "plastic flute" instead.

The Size of the World

On their third day with Sister Mary, Michael Barber reveals that he does not know where Spain is, and Sister Mary slaps a hand to her forehead as if they are too much—just too, too much. And it's true. As a group, they are woefully ignorant about the world. Nenny knows where Spain is but has no idea what goes on there. The pope lives in Italy, which is shaped like a boot. Russia is a paw print smashed into a pane of glass. But it's not enough, because Sister Mary regards them from the front of the room, clearly disturbed, and when she speaks, she chooses her words very carefully so they might understand.

"This," she says, waving her hand to indicate them, the room, "is not the world. The world is very big. We are just a tiny part." She is silent for a moment to let that sink in: you, you precious little beasts, are not the center of the universe.

Then she turns abruptly and begins writing on the board. "Every week you will bring in one item from the news. You will give us the facts and your opinions about them. Everyone will share." She turns back to face them, dusting the chalk off her hands as if chalk, too, was a small disgrace. On the board she has written, in bold block letters, "THE WORLD IS VERY BIG," and below, smaller, "What is our place in it?"

So now they have to give reports. Michael has to go first because he got them into this mess.

"Michael, why don't you begin?" Sister says calmly the following week, as though ready to forgive their collective stupidity and start anew.

Michael walks to the front of the room. He is a very awkward boy, the kind of boy whose mother irons his pants every day to no avail. He's messy in a cartoonish sort of way, beyond help.

"On Monday," he begins, "a boat carrying hundreds of barrels of oil crashed in Alaska. It was a disaster! There was oil everywhere. Oil in the water. Oil on the ducks! Will they ever be able to clean up all that oil? I guess only history will tell." He lets his hands drop to his sides and smiles expectantly. The room's as quiet as an empty box.

"And..." Sister Mary says, her eyebrows raised.

"And that's all." Michael shrugs. "I guess history will tell."

"Michael," Sister says, with the gentle patience of trying to teach something to a two-celled organism. "Where's your article?"

He flips his paper over as if it will miraculously be attached, then shrugs. "My house?" as a question, as if someone else might know.

Sister Mary blinks and takes a deep, deep breath. "Thank you, Michael. You may return to your seat." She stands at the board, deep in thought. After a pause, she writes, "Who What Where When Why How."

"Let's try again," she says patiently. It's obvious she'd do anything to have another adult in the room, someone to nod vigorously and say *Yes, it is crazy making, isn't it?* "Each week you will bring in an article from a newspaper or magazine. The article *must* be stapled to the back of your report"—she doesn't glance at Michael, but the rest of them do—"and cannot be from the *Citrus Times*." A small murmur moves through the room, because clearly they've all referred to the *Citrus Times*. "Why can't it be from the *Citrus Times*?" Sister asks, anticipating their idiocy. "Because the purpose of this assignment is to understand the scope of the world." She pauses so that anyone may write that down, which Katie Marion—and only Katie Marion—eagerly does. "Finally, when you present, you must answer these basic questions in your report. Who, what, where, when, why, and how. For example, Michael might have told us, who was the captain of the ship? What caused the crash? When did the accident happen—during the day, or at night when most of the crew was asleep? And so on." Michael nods eagerly, as if the answer to all of those questions is yes. "Any questions?"

Jessica raises her hand. "My family only gets the *Citrus Times*..." and trails off, as if it's hopeless, there's nothing she can do.

"That's fine. I'll bring in extra papers and leave them here. Anyone may come in during lunch. Any other questions?"

No, there are no other questions. If they thought they could skirt through the third grade thinking only of themselves, well, clearly they were wrong.

Daddy's Boy

THE FEBRUARY 27 issue of *Time* magazine features a painting of a man with a big white beard and eyes so deep it's impossible to discern if they're kind or cruel. The cover reads "The Ayatollah Orders a Hit" in bold, threatening yellow. Nenny has no idea what any of that means, but a report due is a report due.

"Can I have this?" she asks Dad, who's in the kitchen making beans & franks. All their meals are linked with ampersands: beans & franks, spaghetti & meatballs, macaroni & cheese. It's the divorced-dad fare. Cheap & not good for you, but tasty & easy to prepare.

"Let's see that," he says, goofily taking the magazine. He holds it up to his nose as if he can't see the print. When Dad cooks, he becomes excitable, happy for company and distraction. It's actually not difficult to discern his moods. If you want something, try to catch him when he's cooking or folding laundry or, really, doing any chore. If you're looking to piss him off, tap his shoulder when he's driving or, better, knock on the bathroom door. Bug him when he's grading papers if you want to be ignored. That's really the best and the worst time: you can effectively get and do what you want, but have you ever been ignored? Or been nine and ignored?

"You're reading *Time* now? Baby-Sitters Club not informative enough?"

You know what I read? Nenny is so delighted he's picked up on this detail that she ignores the jab.

"It's for school," she says. "Sister Mary's making us do reports."

"Good for her." He starts flipping through the pages. After a minute, he shakes his head mournfully and lays the magazine in front of her. "Messy stuff," he says and sighs then, a heavy and distressed sigh. If she could, she'd just bring Dad to school and have him sigh like that in front of the class. His sigh illustrates perfectly the size of the world, that it is very, very big.

The article about the ayatollah is long and hard to understand. It's filled with words she's never seen before, so she gives up before the end of the third paragraph. She flips to the letters at the front. There seems to be a lot of back-and-forth about last month's issue. One guy writes, "There is no reason a private citizen should have need for a semiautomatic rifle." A guy from Portugal is upset about luxury bunkers in Japan: "Who wants to live underground like a mole?" Nenny flips and flips. There's an article called "The Immigration Mess," accompanied by a photo of people waiting in an endless, hot-looking line. A complicated chart details the trial of some guy named Oliver North. At the bottom of page 20 she spies a tiny article, Dad shouts, "Dinner!" and she decides whatever it's about, it's good enough.

—∿—

"Encouraged by his father's success as president, George W. Bush is considering a run for governor," Nenny reads the next morning, standing in front of the class.

"Nenny, if I may," Sister Mary says from where she's leaning on her desk. She rarely sits at it. She tends to lean against this side of it so that at any moment she can scribble something on the board or circle the room with big gestures. "Rather than reading, would you please summarize the article in your own words?"

"Okay." Nenny glances at the article, then says, "Basically, President Bush's son wants to be governor, but nobody likes him."

"Nobody likes him?"

"Yeah, no one would vote for him." She glances at the page. "He told a bunch of his friends to ask around about his"— glance—"chances for winning, but they don't look good."

"Interesting." Sister nods and looks at the class to see if they agree. They don't. "Does the article say why?"

Nenny looks down again. All she wants to do is sleep, to just sleep through a whole night with no images or dreams or sounds. "They say he's just running as Prince George, and Texans don't like that kind of thing."

"Good. And what do you think?"

Nenny considers the article. It's called "Daddy's Boy" and has a little photo of George Jr. on it. He looks handsome but smug, like even in the photo you can tell he's sure he'll win. Nenny shrugs. "It seems like he's just running because his dad is president. And . . ." She thinks. "I don't know. That seems like a dumb reason to run for governor." She's not even sure what a governor does, but it probably requires more qualifications than just being the president's son.

"Okay. Thank you, Nenny," Mary says, and Nenny returns to her seat. Everyone looks terrifically bored. Is this how you measure the size of the world? In drowsy eyes and stifled yawns? The next day Sister Mary hands her article back. On it, she's written, "Nice work. In the future, don't be afraid to choose bigger articles," and given Nenny a B.

Leonard

ON THOSE rare nights when she does sleep, Nenny dreams things
no one should have to dream, certainly not a child. Sideways
things, abstract things—bloodied teeth at the back of a mouth,
or the sun nearing the earth so close they all shrivel up and die.
One night she dreams of an angel with bricks for a face, rattling
a stick covered in glass bones.

"Daddy?" Tiny says at breakfast, slurping Chex from a
spoon. "Who's that man in the alley?"

"Man in the alley?"

"Yeah. The one with all them cans."

"Cans?" Dad says and looks at Bubbles. Since Bubbles is the
oldest, he's often tasked with translation. But Bubbles just shrugs
and goes back to his cereal.

"The man with the cans," Nenny says, because she's seen and
heard him too. Late at night, long after everyone's in bed, a man
who is no more than a shadow from her second-story window
pushes a shopping cart down the alley behind Citrus Grove,
stopping at the bins to pull out bottles and cans. It's like a song
played each night: the clatter of his cart, thump of a bin's lid,

sounds of rummaging, glass breaking other glass, thump of lid, clatter, clatter, noise fading, gone. "The bottles and cans."

"Oh!" Dad says, as if she's transcribed ancient Hebrew when all she did was repeat what Tiny said. "That's Leonard."

"Leonard?" Tiny says, squinting and confused.

"Yeah, Leonard. The homeless guy," as if this is a complete description of a man.

Homeless. The word hangs over the table, hovering in the air. Nenny pictures Leonard beneath the canopy of a broken tent, using a pocketknife to open a can of beans, then realizes that everything she knows about homeless people comes from cartoons: trash-can fires and fingerless gloves, fishing for boots, that sort of thing.

Tiny, though, clearly doesn't get it. "Where does he live?" he asks between bites.

"He doesn't live anywhere," Dad says. "He's homeless."

Tiny stops, spoon stilled midair. His eyes twitch slightly at the corners and his lower lip juts out. It's clear this concept, as a possibility, has never occurred to him before.

Now Nenny translates Dad for Tiny. "Homeless people don't have homes. They sleep outside."

Tiny turns to Nenny then, a long look on his face. This goes on for a full minute, and Nenny prepares herself to answer his questions about the ways of the world. She's older, she's wiser, she knows things. War happens and people kill each other. They'll look you right in your face and say awful, heartless things. This life is not easy, Tiny. People will hurt you and trample you, they'll fixate on your weaknesses, belittle and diminish your dreams. People you love will lie right to your face. You'll be betrayed, stampeded, threatened, told where you come from and exactly where you can go. You think anybody cares what happens to you? Sure, they love you now, they take care of you now—but just wait a few years. Wait till your adorable charm wears off. Then you'll see what it's really all about. There is no such thing as *grace*, Tiny. There is no *mercy*. It's just you and everyone else against one another. It's a brutal and unforgiving world.

But then, before she's had a chance to explain, he says, out of nowhere, "I caughted a caterpillar yesterday at school," and that's the end of that.

Display

Weekends back at Mom's feel like clamps around your ribs, or a firm grip on your head. Things have changed, and the differences are so subtle it's like water at your toes, rising imperceptibly to swallow you up. On a small table in their room, Kat has set up what can only be called a shrine: a black-and-white photo of Windsor (her hair pulled back, wearing an unfocused and wistful gaze) floats among a sea of loose beads and dried flowers left over from the funeral. Kat refers to her now as "Mom" openly and without reservation, whereas before Windsor's death the word was like a stone in her mouth, like dirt. But now she says it all the time, at every opportunity—"I found Mom's old diary" or "I dreamt about Mom again"—as though Windsor is everyone's mom, as though everyone wants to talk about their mom who is dead.

Charles, on the other hand, is as fixed as a tomb. There's no writing in his diary like the counselor suggests, no sudden floods of tears. There's just Charles, stony and closed. It's as if someone has come along and built a wall smack through the middle of Kensington Drive, and on one side grief is loud and colorful and open, filled with memories and hot, wet tears; on the other, it's as grey and lifeless as a concrete slab. It doesn't matter, really, which side you are on. Either, both, could puncture you, shred you in two.

—⁓—

Sunday morning, Kat comes thumping up the stairs with a box from the garage. "Look what I found," she says triumphantly and starts emptying it on the bed. "It's Mom's old belly-dancing clothes."

Nenny had no idea that Windsor was a dancer, let alone a belly-dancing one. She tries to picture Windsor on a stage under a spotlight, but all she sees is that leather jacket and her jagged teeth, men throwing cans at the stage like in a cartoon.

The box is filled with all kinds of bangles and jangles, silver and gold bracelets, skirts that touch the floor. Kat pulls them out and examines each one like a museum piece. Her back is to Nenny; she's facing the mirrored closet, which takes up a whole wall.

"She used to have this sword, this belly-dancing sword," Kat says, laying things on the bed, "and Charles tried to swallow it. Sliced the roof of his mouth." She turns to Nenny and points inside her mouth.

The questions arrive in a stampede. When was Windsor a belly dancer? Before or after they were born? Is that how Rick met her? At a belly-dancing show? What was the sword for? How old was Charles when he tried to swallow it? Who tries to swallow a *sword*, for criminy's sake?

She would've answered too, Nenny knows it—this is one of those moments, one of those rare sister moments—but then

Kat suddenly does something unexpected: she begins to take off her clothes. She does it quickly, without unease, as if it's nothing, as if they undress in front of each other all the time. But the thing is, they don't. Nenny takes her clothes with her to the bathroom in the morning and does the same when it's time for bed. It's a tacit agreement they have, where privacy is an intricate game with unyielding rules. Nenny walked in on Kat once, when she was in the bathroom. All she was doing was curling her hair, but she looked at Nenny with fury in her eyes and said, "Do you *mind?*" as if curling one's hair is the most intimate and sacred of acts.

Now Kat stands with her back to Nenny, in just her panties and bra, holding Windsor's clothes to her frame and turning in the mirror. Of course Nenny's seen Kat in a bathing suit before, but this feels different somehow. Her skin is pocked and white, more textured than Nenny would've imagined it to be. There are freckles on her thighs and hips, shocking for their color and size, as if someone has pressed their fingers into her and left marks. Nenny's own skin is suddenly flushed, a hot swirl of anxious strain. She's being invited to look as if looking's no big deal, but she does not know where to settle her eyes.

In the mirror, Nenny's face is blank, like a flower that will never do anything, never open or even close. She stands up and hurriedly grabs her shoes. "I'm going outside." But why? To do what? Kat doesn't watch her go. She's in her own world, turning in that mirror, ever so slow.

The Thing About Fear

THE THING about fear that no one tells you is that it's like the cup in the myth about Thor: you can drink and drink and you will never be done. Fastidiously, steadily, without consciousness, you can devote everything you have to being afraid. Through dedication—or mere habit, really—fear becomes as hardwired within you as the length of your scrawny limbs or the color of your turd-brown eyes. Fear doesn't just define you, fear *is* you: your breath, your eyes, your ears, your mouth. *You* are the house ablaze. You are the earth being torn apart. You are the masked men, their hunger, their rage. You are the vacant eyes of what really happened in Vietnam.

Until something real happens. When something real happens, you're not even afraid anymore. Brittle, maybe, or a little coarse. Fear leaves and a kind of anger settles in its place. And you know what? There was never any point! The sleepless nights, the churning in your gut, the gnawed-down fingernails—what a waste! Because the most frightening thing possible will never even occur to you. If anything, *that's* what you should fear. That you will never, ever anticipate the thing that all along you should have feared the most.

Confession

SISTER RENATA must've begun sowing seeds for what is to come—Communion, confirmation, a lifetime of sit and kneel and stand—because all of a sudden Tiny's obsessed with the holy rite of confession. It's all he wants to talk about, pummeling Dad with questions. What do they say in the confession booth? How come a priest is the only one to forgive? What if the priest says no?

"The priest never says no."

"But what if he does?"

"He doesn't, Tiny. You'll always be forgiven, as long as you confess."

Tiny gets his hands on two large boxes (Mrs. Anderson in 7G got a new oven and fridge) and spends the afternoon taping them together and cutting holes. He begs Dad for an old sheet, insists that it be white, then takes scissors and trims it down.

Nenny's sitting by the pool when he approaches. He looks ridiculous, like exactly what he is: a six-year-old in a bedsheet robe playing priest. It's the kind of moment parents adore, taking snapshots to cherish for years—*You were so cute in your little robe*—but Dad doesn't take snapshots of anything.

"My child," Tiny says, hands touching at his chest, "come confess your sins."

"No thanks," Nenny says, as if he's offered her gum. Panic flashes across his face. He glances back at his booth, then around at the empty yard, the lifeless pool. There's no one else to confess.

He turns back to Nenny, his eyes sad, a boy with no one to forgive. "Pwease," he begs, and since Boots went somewhere with her mom, and it's boring under the canopy of palms, and Nenny knows what it feels like to reach and have no one there, she stands and dusts off her pants.

"Fine," she says, clipping the word so he'll know what a huge favor this is.

"Yay!" he shrieks and starts to run across the yard.

"Priests don't run," she calls, and he grinds to a halt, walking solemnly the rest of the way.

When she gets there, he politely holds the cardboard door open for her. She doesn't bother to tell him the priest should already be *inside*. What's the point of confession if the priest has seen your face? The whole point is you can go in there and spill your stupid sinful guts and the priest won't look at you funny next time at church.

Nenny wriggles her way into the box. She must admit, given his limited resources, he's done an impressive job of approximating a confessional. He's cut the bottom flaps so the boxes rest flat on the ground and run tape along their edges so they share a common wall. He's cut two corresponding mouth-level holes in each box, his version of the sliding windows in the booth. A plastic crate acts as a stool. Nenny sits and waits for Tiny to settle on the other side. The booth rustles with his movement, as if disturbed by a slight wind, and then, finally, he takes a deep breath, preparing for his role.

"My child, why have you come?" He asks this calmly and without judgment, almost lovingly, and she wonders what movie he got this from. He's certainly never been to confession before. You're not allowed to until at least second grade.

"I came because you made me," Nenny says. She feels his confusion as a slight stir in the box, and then his mouth is at the hole, whispering, breaking the fourth wall.

"No, you sposed to say 'Bless me, Father, for I have sinned,'" he instructs.

I know, stupid, she thinks, but sighs and plays along.

"Bless me, Father, for I have sinned," she recites robotically.

He settles back. "And what, my child, is your sin?"

Nenny glances around the box, her lips pursed. She's always hated confession. What a joke. You sit in some dank box in front of a little window so the priest can't see your face and you can't see his, but come on—there's only so many priests to choose from. If the box reeks like booze, it's Father Chauncey; if he's quiet and lets you do all the talking, Father Bill. It's not rocket science to figure out who's who. And then you're supposed to confess your sins, but what sins? Not listening in class? Thinking Katie Marion's stupid? And then the priest makes the sign of the cross and tells you to count some beads? Please.

"Um, I littered," Nenny says.

"You littered?" Tiny's clearly unsure if littering's a sin, and his confusion is justified because it's probably not.

"Yeah. I threw a can in a lake or something. At a duck."

"You throwed a can at a duck?"

"Uh-huh," and as she says it, Nenny kind of wishes she had. Who knew pretend confession was as boring as real confession.

"You shouldn't throw cans at ducks. That's a sin."

"I know. That's why I said it."

He's silent a minute. Evidently his pretend time in the pretend seminary didn't quite prepare him for this. "What else?"

"What else what?"

"What other sins?" he asks, tacking on a "my child" as an afterthought.

Suddenly, out of nowhere, something crackles within her. It's scorching white, and she hates Tiny and wants to hurt him. She feels mean, vengeful—things should be getting better, but they're not. Everyone should be coming together through their sadness like they do on TV, to form something warmer and close-knit, but they aren't. It's a sin to say what she's about to say, but it'd be a sin not to.

She leans close to the hole. "I killed someone."

Tiny's silence is hot and immediate and fierce. "You what?"

"I killed someone. I shot him and left him to die."

The air in the box is suddenly consumed. *That's what you get,* she thinks, but who knows who she's talking to anymore. *Ashes to ashes, you stupid jerks.*

A quiet as big as rocks falling.

"No," Tiny finally says. He's only six years old, for criminy's sake. Maybe that's the biggest sin of all. "Do a different one."

"A different what?"

"A different sin." His voice sounds stricken.

Nenny sighs. A game is just a game is just a game until it's not a game anymore. "I lied. My sin is I lied."

"About what?" Father Tiny says somewhat hopefully, on the verge of forgiveness but also unsure.

"I didn't kill anyone," she admits.

"And the duck?"

"Yeah, I lied about that too."

"Okay, good," he says, pleased. "Say one hundred Hail Marys."

"That's too many," Nenny says.

"It is?"

"Yeah."

Pause. "Okay. Say ten."

After that, he doesn't ask about confession anymore.

Rampage

It's BEEN almost three months since Windsor died and nothing changes, nothing's changing. Everything is shrouded in a terrible mist, everyone floating in their own separate worlds. Tiny makes stuff up, perhaps to escape things as they really are, and Bubbles acts as if the solution lies buried in the guts of some toaster or clock radio. Dad behaves as though he doesn't know what's going on. On weekends, Kat is like a ballerina trapped in a box, like a person dancing slowly and sadly to music only she can hear. Mom is distant these days, and there's no understanding or penetrating Rick. Charles won't even talk to Nenny, not at home and not at school. "You'll see each other at school," Mom'd said, but what happens if no one sees you? What happens if you do not know how to be seen?

It's Tuesday, and Sister Mary is telling the story of Jesus on the mount. He's up there praying because he's scared; all anyone ever does in these stories is pray. That said, Mary does know how to weave a tale. She holds a captive audience, sketching with words the night in the olive grove, small pebbles digging into Jesus's knees, slow clouds moving across a moonlit sky. Tomorrow Jesus will be crucified, and though they know this story like the backs of their hands, everyone is on the edge of their seats.

Everyone except Nenny. Nenny doesn't care about Jesus on the mount. Last night the phone rang, and since no one ever calls, Bubbles asked, "Who was that?" after Dad hung up.

"Your mom," Dad said, back in his paper-grading chair.

"What?" Nenny said, and they all looked at him. "What did she say?"

"Oh, she had a question about tuition or something," Dad said, having already forgotten a conversation that took place literally two seconds ago. Why didn't Mom ask to talk to them? Why didn't he pass the phone around? It didn't occur to either of them that they might want to talk to their *mom?* Nenny sits at her desk in the circle, doodling squares inside of squares, distracted and a little sick, because someone—anyone—is supposed to be captain of this ship, but they just keep running the ship aground.

The lead in her pencil snaps, she's pressing so hard. Before, with Sister Timothy, you had to raise your hand to sharpen your pencil, you had to raise your hand for everything—permission to use the bathroom, permission to get a drink of water—but Mary lets them do things without raising their hands. Nenny rises from her desk and goes to the sharpener by the window.

Outside, the sky is a burnished blue, the playground empty, the flag lying still at the top of the pole, while in here, Jesus is waiting for Judas to show up and betray him. Nenny puts her pencil in the sharpener and turns the handle, and then happens to glance at Mary's face. A look passes there, a quick blink and a furrow of her brow.

Nenny glances at her teacher's face and sees that the sharpening sound has made her lose her place. She thinks, *Well, that was easy.* She returns to her desk. The story drags on, it's been the same story for years, a bag of silver and three rooster crows, and Nenny digs her pencil into the page and presses so hard it snaps again. She says, "Oops!" loud enough for everyone to hear. She rises and goes to the sharpener and waits for the look, waits for Mary's irritation or scorn, anything, and understands, in some way, why Steve Smoot eats paper and Donnie Harlem is such a jerk all the time—anything to attract a gaze.

"Nenny?" Mary says, pausing the story. "Is everything okay?"

"My pencil keeps breaking." Nenny's standing at the sharpener and has no idea what's happening inside her, but it's a sour mix of disappointment and inertia and everything feeling locked. It's a hateful, reckless thing, and she loves it. "This pencil is a piece of crap."

There's an audible intake of breath, and everyone is stunned. Katie Marion looks as though she's been slapped. Obviously Nenny's blurted stuff out before, but never a bad word, never like this—like stabbing something midair. Michelle Wynne puts her hand over her mouth and stifles a laugh.

"Nenny," Mary warns.

Nenny shrugs. "What? It is."

"Please return to your seat," Sister says, with a sternness she's never shown.

Look at that: Nenny's made a nice nun mad.

—⁂—

Of course when the bell rings, Sister calls her name to stay behind. Nenny anticipated as much. Everyone else shuffles out, not even pretending not to stare. Nenny prepares herself for nun

234 · ZULEMA RENEE SUMMERFIELD

wrath—Old World, Cold War kind of nun wrath. Nun wrath is red-faced and blazing bloodshot eyes. In the movies, it's a ruler to your knuckles or whips on your behind, but it's 1989 and that kind of barbarism simply doesn't fly anymore. Now nun wrath is fifty Hail Marys or having to recite the Apostles' Creed at the front of the room, which they're all supposed to know by heart but no one does. It's thrusting the hall pass into your hands and telling you to "March," and you don't have to be told where to go. It's sitting in Mother Superior's office, your legs swinging, your shoes knocking against the chair. It's Mother Superior getting Mother More Superior on the phone. "Nenny," she says, that one word enough. The message is crystal clear: *Knock it off. There's a time and a place, and Sacred Heart school is neither of those.*

But nun wrath is not what Mary delivers. Instead, she pulls a desk close to Nenny's and sits.

"Shall we talk?" Mary says. She doesn't seem angry anymore. Nenny doesn't know what to do, so she just shrugs. A talk is not what she expected. A lecture, maybe, but not a talk, desks close and everyone else outside.

"How are you? Is everything okay?" And Nenny thinks, *No, things are definitely not okay,* but can't bear to look at Mary because her anger, her defiance, have dissolved in the dust-specked room. There's no way to articulate any of it, how horrible things are, how much she misses Mom, how small and invisible she feels, so she shrugs again, a little shoulder bounce.

Mary doesn't press for an answer, just nods. She has her hands folded on the desk. If this were a movie, her hands would be soft and elegant, with little pink fingernails. But this isn't a movie, it's real life, and Sister's hands are bumpy and rough like a man's hands. A small scar runs the length of her forefinger. It's hard not to notice that scar.

"What's that?" Nenny asks, though questions about scars and things are rude. When she was seven, there was a man at the mall who did not have a nose, just a hole in his face where his nose should have been. When Nenny pointed, Mom slapped her hand and pulled her into the bathroom at Macy's. "Why would you do that? Why would you be so rude?" she said, shaking Nenny by the arm. And it was so sudden, so strange, Mom so angry that it might as well have been a hole in her own face, her own parts missing or deformed. Nenny did not know then—who knows if she even knows it now?—that there's a distinction between curiosity and cruelty, though the space between them is slight.

This feels different, though. If the man at the mall had been sitting with her in a quiet room, asking how things are, she probably could have asked about his nose. Why a noseless man would be sitting with her is beside the point. The point is, she could have asked.

Sister Mary holds her finger up and peers at it, as if only now remembering the scar is there. "A can opener," she says. "I took the knife part out to open a can—I was quite young—and *schlip!*" She makes a motion with her other hand and laughs. "My father was very mad."

Mary looks up from her hand and out the window and says, out of nowhere, "You know what I do when I'm sad?" She looks back at Nenny then and nods, like *Yep, even nuns get sad.* "I do this little exercise. I look around at people on the street and imagine that God is living in each of them. I think, God is that woman walking her dog. God is that woman with a cane. God is that angry little boy." Mary points at her imaginary crowd. "God is him, and God is him, and God is her. And then, when I am at my most sad"—she closes her eyes, lays her hands on her chest, takes a deep breath—"I think, God is here too. Right here."

She sits like that for a few long seconds, breathing and with her hands folded on her chest, but when she opens her eyes, she must see the skepticism on Nenny's face, because she sighs and says, "Okay. That's probably enough talking for today. You can go play."

But no. Nenny remains glued to her seat, her eyes fixed on the desk, and doesn't say anything, just stays where she is.

"No? You want to stay?"

Nenny doesn't nod, but she doesn't not nod either, and what occurs to her then could break your heart, if only a little: Sister Mary is not robotically rattling her name off roll, and she's not scolding Nenny in front of the class. She's not calling her Nelly by mistake, not shaking her head and saying, "You think it's funny? So funny to be a clown?" Instead, she's sitting in an empty classroom with Nenny, trying to show her where God lives. *That* he lives.

Hot tears collect on the ledges of Nenny's eyelids, and Sister says nothing but lays one hand, one perfectly deformed hand, across Nenny's back. Recess goes on for a long while, it seems, all the other kids yelping and hollering outside.

Exercise

Imagine God as recently divorced. He sleeps sprawled on the couch, one arm slung over his face, snoring like a broken machine. In the morning, God wakes in his shorts and rubs his eyes, his face sleep-dented and grooved. He goes into the kitchen and stands at the sink, his grip white at its edge, grimacing because pain is blitzing his spine. Imagine that's God making breakfast, aching with every ounce to be cheerful for your sake, to ignore the agony in his spine.

Or God is your best friend, and she lives with her mother in 3G. God is just nine years old, and already she's got a solid grasp on things. When you walk with God to Thrifty's after school, she does an impression of Alf that's so spot-on you almost burst from laughing, steadying yourself against a stone wall while all the jerks driving by slow down to stare. God is the only person you know who orders pecan praline ice cream.

Or God is your best friend's mother, who teaches first grade at a public school forty-five minutes away—with traffic, an hour or more. When God's husband left, she took her daughter to live in the mountains, because she thought it'd be good for her, all that fresh mountain air. Once they got there, though, God found there was no work, really, so she took a job at a diner called Lou's, worked the late shift, and prayed nothing would happen to her kid, alone in some creaky mountain house. Now, when she comes home from work, God sits in her car and leans the seat all the way back, and stays like that for a long time, listening to the afternoon shows on NPR.

Or God is your little brother, and he squirms in his chair when he has to poop. He watches *Pee-wee's Playhouse* from his blanket fort and says "please" like "pweas." One day he tells Boots about Manny—"Manny Hernandez, one time he caughted a owl, and he put it in a box, and the owl laided three eggs, but in the morning there was only *two* eggs, even though Manny putted a big rock on the lid"—and Boots listens and nods because she's not related to him and also because Boots is nice. "Where does Manny live?" she asks, and God blinks and kind of shakes his head. "He doesn't live nowhere," somewhat impatiently, as though it's her question and not his answer that doesn't make sense.

Or God is Bubbles, who eats cold hot dogs dipped in sour cream and pours ketchup on his mac and cheese. He takes the wheels off his bike just to stare at the spokes, makes a battery out of a potato, looks confounded when he ties his shoes. He wants an electric drill for his birthday.

Or God is Mr. Wilder in 6G, who smokes on his porch and has a cat named Pushkin. Or Mrs. Carter, whose husband works overseas. The Garcia boys, chalk-drawing robots and spaceships in the parking lot when they get home from school. The couple who lives at the end of the building, him with a wild grey moustache and her with tattoos running down her arms like sleeves. Or maybe Mr. Baldy: imagine God is Chuck

Baldy, with a paunch like a great big pillow under his shirt and probably—though it's difficult to fathom—a good reason for *still* not cleaning the pool. Or Leonard, with all his bottles and cans.

Or this, try this: imagine God is you. Nenny lies in the bathtub and submerges her head up to her ears and lets her hands float numbly at her sides. She listens to the muted thrum of the world underwater and does as Mary suggested, which is to imagine that God occupies a space inside her. She breathes deep, as Mary did, her body gently buoyed with each breath, and stays like that a long time. A warmth begins to spread through her like light, and she lets it be, does not question or disrupt it, and something happens then, something arrives, a new feeling like crawling back from somewhere far away.

Hail Mary

FRIDAY, THE third grade's day for confession. Nenny finds a pew near the back of the church and folds the kneeler down. On Sundays it's impossible to concentrate, so many people and so much noise, itchy tights and pinching shoes, Tiny rolling around like a bug in the pew—but on Fridays she sometimes feels as though she is all alone. She takes out her rosary to pray, then closes her eyes.

Hail Mary, full of grace, the Lord is with thee. Blessed art thou among women, and blessed is the fruit of thy womb, Jesus. Holy Mary, mother of God, pray for us sinners, now and at the hour of our death. Amen.

Hail Mary, full of grace, the Lord is with thee. Blessed art thou among women, and blessed is the fruit of thy womb, Jesus. Holy Mary, mother of God, pray for us sinners, now and at the hour of our death. Amen.

Hail Mary, full of grace, the Lord is with thee. Blessed art thou among women—*but how many women?* Nenny suddenly thinks, and her hands go numb on the beads. Without meaning to, she pictures Windsor that last day in the van. Improbably, but beautifully, she's wearing her belly-dancing clothes: a long green-gold skirt billows in the wind coming through the window, the sun catching on a belt of coins. The dusty, ancient smell of a Catholic church, but in all that silence and echoing, it's hard—impossible—not to think of the desert in midday, a sandaled foot pressing pedals to the floor. Here is a thing that Nenny is only now beginning to learn, an inglorious lesson to take with her for her whole life: if a person you know or sort of know dies, you fixate on the most minor, insignificant things. What was the last thing she ate? The last thing she said? The last thing she saw? Was there a song playing on the radio that day in the van? Nenny's mind flashes to the song she heard in the car with Rick: *He rich. Is he rich like me?* The echoes from other pews. If a person dies in a movie, they see their whole life flash before them—births, weddings, sunrises, a kid on a swing—but is that really true? How would anyone know? The only people who know that are already—*Hail Mary*. Nenny can't help it: she thinks of Windsor thinking of her babies, their tiny hands, their hair soft as down, and something snags and claws inside her. In those final moments, what are the things that matter most? What are the things that bind you when you are terribly, irrevocably bound?

Hail Mary, full of grace.
Hail Mary, Hail Mary, Hail Mary.

When Someone Dies

SATURDAY MORNING at Mom's there's an illustrated book on the coffee table called *When Someone Dies,* by Laura Hofstader, PhD. It's just sitting there as if it waltzed in of its own accord or (*Look at that!*) fell from the sky, but everyone knows it's Mom's doing. They all must see it when they come downstairs—sitting in the middle of the coffee table like a brick—but no one mentions it. Mom cooks eggs and hash browns and doesn't say a word. Rick is quiet too, which leads Nenny to believe that he's in on it somehow. *Who knows? Maybe one of the kids will pick it up?* Gain a little unforced, subtle insight into this haunting, foreboding thing called death. By the end of breakfast, the book's presence is like a low hum coming from the other room. Midmorning, the hum has become a thrum. A raucous shout by the end of the afternoon. Nenny can't stand it anymore. She snatches the book from the table and locks herself in the bathroom upstairs with it.

"All living things, including animals and bugs and people," begins Laura Hofstader, PhD, "die." Death is a part of life, hard as it is to understand. "Where do dead people go?" Many people believe that when we die it's just our bodies that die, that there's another part of us that lives forever, "our *spirit* or our *soul.*" Something about a broken glass of water but the water still remains. Honestly, Nenny's not really paying attention anymore. She flips to the back. There's a list addressed to parents there ("Be honest. Encourage questions. Allow yourself to cry."), which feels conspicuous and lame, like grown-ups talking about you in the third person even though you're standing right there. She tucks the book back under her shirt and returns it to the table downstairs.

Mom is in the kitchen, cutting vegetables at the sink. Nenny looks at her back, the unwashed, matted aspect of her hair. Laura Hofstader, PhD, failed to mention something else, something crucial, this: what it means to be the parent of a child whose other parent has died. Nenny goes to Mom and hugs her from behind, arms around her waist and cheek pressed into her back, and feels what all creatures, at some point, must feel: to swallow and be swallowed, to eat what you love whole.

Bundle

THE NEXT day, just before dinner, the strangest thing happens—Gabe shows up. Or maybe "strange" is not the word. Maybe the word does not exist.

Mom's cooking and Kat has volunteered to help, which is common practice these days. Kat offers to help, she doesn't talk back anymore, she doesn't snort or roll her eyes, her outfits have toned down, sweatshirts and jeans and no makeup at all—and she acts like it's no big deal, like it's been like this all along, when in fact there's not a single one of them who hasn't noticed the change and felt it for what it is, which is seismic and a little frightening. If losing her mother could so transform Kat, and in such a cosmically minuscule amount of time, how would a similar loss transform each of them? It's scary to think of what you are, what you might or might not become.

"Do you like cooking?" Mom asks Kat. She's at the counter, chopping onions, and talks to Kat in this formal, investigatory way, like trying to find common ground with some stranger who appears in your kitchen one day.

"I think so. I might take home ec next semester with Leah."

When the doorbell rings, everyone's in their place, like in a play: Rick's watching the news in the den and Charles is slumped near him in a beanbag chair, a comic held close to his face; Mom and Kat are in the kitchen, bonding or whatever; Nenny's at the table, trying to read; and Tiny and Bubbles are both upstairs, doing who knows what.

The doorbell rings and Rick mutes the TV. He says, "Got it," as though expecting someone, though of course he's not. He opens the door and says something like "Hey, there" or "How are you?" in a way that is reserved and a little slow, a way that, even from where she's sitting at the table, Nenny can tell means it's not a neighbor or a friend.

Gabe looks utterly destroyed. His cheeks look carved, as if someone's worked away too furiously at unstable stone. At Rick's invitation he comes in and stands at the entrance to the dining room, seeming underfed and confused. He carries a big blue bundle in his arms.

"These are some things," he starts to say, before Charles steps out from the TV room to see who it is. In quick succession Charles's mouth drops open and then closes again, his jaw sets and his eyes turn to steel, and then he stomps upstairs to his room and slams the door. Gabe's eyes follow him dully.

"What are you doing here?" Kat asks, not trying to be rude, but of course it is. Mom says, "Kat," but doesn't look at her, just stands staring at Gabe as she uses a towel to dry her hands.

"Your mom had these," Gabe starts, lifting the bundle weakly. He blinks long and heavy and starts again. "They were for Christmas, for you for Christmas." He pauses, as if unsure if this is true, or if Christmas is even a thing. "And Charles," he adds, glancing toward the stairs.

Rick steps forward to take the bundle, and right then Nenny

notices Tiny and Bubbles on the landing at the top of the stairs. Everyone's staring, waiting for the show to begin.

But it doesn't, really, or anyway it's not much of a show. If they've come to expect wild, drunken antics from movies and TV—the widower raging in his grief, smashing things and throwing punches, howling, collapsing on the floor—that's not what this is at all. Gabe, unkempt and unwashed and thin and probably recently very, very drunk in a way that he will be again and again, stands frozen in the dining room, looking for all the world like he doesn't know where he'll go to next or what in God's name he'll do when he arrives.

"Thank you, Gabe," Mom says, and for a brief second Nenny wonders if she'll invite him to dinner. It's the kind of thing Mom would do—extend a branch and all that. But strangely she doesn't, and neither does Rick, and in their silence, everyone—all of them—becomes suddenly aware of where their loyalties lie, and it's not with Gabe. Probably someone, Rick maybe, should see him out to his car, touch his shoulder or his arm if not in a loving way then at least in a human way, acknowledge somehow that the death of Windsor was his loss too—but no one does. Once he goes, they'll never see him again. He could be dead or living still, who knows. It's hard to say if anyone cares.

—⁓—

The bundle, in fact, consists of just two things. The first is a dream catcher, likely not authentically made, but still, it's beautiful. The hoop is woven with gold and black thread and adorned with turquoise beads. Three delicate blue feathers hang from the bottom. Clearly, it's intended for Kat. Mom hands it to her without a word, and everyone watches as she turns it over in her hands, marveling as if it's the only thing of its kind ever made, though you could probably find one just like it at the gas station down the road. There's a little manufacturer's card tied to it.

"What does it say?" Mom quietly asks. Kat is having a moment, and there's not a single one of them who doesn't appreciate her letting them watch.

"It says, 'Hang this dream catcher above your bed and it will capture all your bad dreams.'" She hiccups, a small, emotional breath, as though Windsor had written the words herself, though obviously she didn't. They all watch quietly as she cries. It takes Rick a good minute to embrace her in a hug, and that's only after Mom gives him a nudge.

The second gift in the bundle would surprise, if only because you would never associate it with Charles. It's a blanket. Sometimes when you're driving you'll see men in sun hats selling blankets out of their vans. They'll take over some empty lot and drape blankets along the surrounding fence—wolves and horses and eagles and a big green plant with five leaves. This one is a sunset, cast in yellow and blue and orange. The sun is a bare round bulb glowing in the center.

But no one gets to see Charles's reaction, because he won't come out of his room. Rick calls, "Charles! He's gone!" but nothing. Even when Rick gently knocks on the door—"There's a present here from your mom"—Charles doesn't make a sound.

—⁂—

Here is a story that is true, a story told only after many years have passed, when Charles and Nenny are grown and friends, sitting around a fire pit in the Santa Cruz Mountains some-where: the summer before Windsor died, Gabe took everyone camping—Windsor, Charles, Kat, his daughter, Becca. He wanted to go to Joshua Tree, which is known as a beautiful but spooky place, filled with massive boulders and epic views of the stars, but also it's the site of strange midnight rituals, and once a guy got his head bashed in while he was sleeping in his tent.

To camp is one thing. To camp with a mean drunk is another entirely. They spent the afternoon scrambling over rocks and eating sandwiches and chips, but everyone knew that the minute the sun dipped past the hills Gabe would switch from beer to whiskey, which he did. He told stories for a while that made Windsor laugh, and that was nice, her sweet bell-like laugh, but then the stories turned to loud boasts and the boasts to silence—hard, angry silence. If you've ever been out to Joshua Tree, then you know what it's like—a breathtaking sky of infi-nite stars but everywhere the threat of misfits or snakes. Finally, Gabe kicked himself up from his camping chair and started lurching around the fire.

He stood over Charles first, his lips and eyes livid and wet, listing sloppily, whiskey clutched in one hand and the other curled into a fist.

"Call me an asshole," Gabe said, drunkenly trying to meet Charles's eyes.

"What?" Charles blinked. He was eight years old.

"I *said*, call me an asshole." He swayed crudely over Charles like a ship in a storm.

Charles looked at Kat, who just looked back. "You're an ass-hole?" he asked more than said and braced himself to be hit with that fist.

But Gabe didn't hit him. Instead, he stumbled over to Kat

and made the same demand—"Call me an asshole"—which she did, no problem, "You're an asshole," and Becca too, "You're an asshole, Dad," both girls looking right at him as they said it, right into his drunk asshole face.

But Windsor wouldn't do it ("I'm not calling you that, Gabe"), not because she wasn't scared—they all were; there was a hole in the wall at home and a gun somewhere in the truck, for Christ's sake—but because, for whatever reason, she loved him. Or maybe love isn't quite it. Maybe it's that she was the kind of person who saw other things, things the rest of us cannot see. That perhaps if she could pry open the buttons on his filthy denim coat she'd discover something else, something glowing past his shame. And maybe that's all she asked in return each time she knelt before her children or chatted with Mom and Rick or gave Nenny and the boys something stupid like a dumb mint—that, however briefly, they'd look through the tassels on her leather coat like peering through a curtain, gaze into her crystal necklace like gazing into a crystal ball, look past the turquoise rings and the shitty car, past the shouting and the abuse and the blame, past the excuses and the stories and the lies and her terrible, awful end, to something else, to whatever else was shining there beneath—shining then, shining still, whatever nugget of self remains.

Ten Amen Square

IN APRIL, fighting breaks out in Namibia—which is a country in Africa—and three hundred people are killed. (To give you a sense of this number, that's every student at Sacred Heart school.) Doctors are still trying to find a cure for the disease called AIDS. Someone tries to take over the country of Haiti, but it doesn't work—this is called a coup, not a coop. Demonstrators for democracy are killed by soldiers in Georgia, and, no, not that Georgia. Sister Mary pulls down the map to explain. On the 15th someone named Hu Yaobang (pronounced "Who Yow Bang") dies in China, and this upsets many people. They begin a series of protests, and by the end of the month they fill the central plaza. It sounds like Ten Amen Square.

In May, Nenny gets a new pair of shoes with two sets of laces, one electric pink and the other neon blue. She goes with Boots and her mom to get library cards, and Bubbles falls from his bike and has to get three stitches in his chin. What else? Not much. Every week there are photos in the paper of the people protesting in China. They are still sleeping in the square.

Massacre

Soon it is the last day of school. How this happened, where time has suddenly gone, is beyond comprehension. There's a noticeable buzz in the air, like there always is on the last day of school. Boys shout more loudly and chase one another more fervently before the bell. Girls gather in small clusters, talking over one another, chattering about summer plans. When the bell rings, they fall into line, but belatedly, just a beat or two delayed. What need have they for bells anymore, or lines, even, or rules? This is all already last year's dream.

Sister Mary, though, is quiet. She taps a pen on her desk as if keeping time, her face unmoving as they make their way into class. Sternness or solemnity, it's hard to say, but there's something hanging in the room like a bank of lights, a mood that's impossible to ignore. Yes, they're largely ignorant; yes, they're willful morons. But even Sacred Heart's third grade can sense a shift in the room.

"Thank you," Mary says when they've finally settled down. She stands and comes around the side of her desk. She's not a tall woman, but her presence is considerable. Nenny looks at her and realizes then that she will miss Sister Mary. She feels this as a dull, mid-body pang, like someone pressing a hand into her gut. Sure, next year Mary will still be here, teaching third grade right next door. But it won't be the same.

"Did anyone see the newspaper this morning?" Sister asks. Everyone glances around. It's the last day of school, there's something in the air, and whatever they've been thinking, that is *not* what they expected her to say.

"Pardon, ma'am?" José asks, on everyone's behalf.

"I asked if you had seen the newspaper today. The photos on the front page?" she repeats. A few students soberly nod their heads, and Nenny knows what Mary is talking about because, as a matter of fact, she did see the paper this morning before school. The photo was of a man, tall and lean and with grocery bags in each of his hands, staring down a line of tanks. For those who missed it, Mary explains: Over the weekend, the Chinese army snuck up on the plaza the class had discussed, stealthily advancing through the midnight streets, creeping up on the students and workers sleeping in their tents—and then opened fire, indiscriminately killing hundreds of people. In the morning, that man stood in front of the tanks, his act a simple one of bravery and defiance and rage.

Sister Mary stands at the front of the room, fixing the entirety of them with her gaze. If Mary's behavior appears at all cruel, that's because it is. Reminding soon-to-be fourth graders of the hard facts of the world, the sheer magnitude of it—especially on the last day of school—is seldom a subtle or gentle task. But each of them, in their own way (except maybe Jackie, who sometimes talks to her own hands), knows by now that the world is a sizeable place, where terrible things happen that are impossible to explain. "Let us keep them in our prayers," Mary says and lets that thought stay in the room for a minute.

Then her voice softens. "All right," she says. "Shall we have a party now? I've brought a cake."

And the party, though it takes a minute to kick off, is pretty fun. Sister lets them pick songs on a stereo she's brought, they play several rounds of charades, Matty and the boys do their standard "La Bamba" lip-sync show. Before the bell, Mary tells them it's been a marvelous year and thanks them for being in her class. There is one thing that Nenny will miss the most, though impossible to articulate or even, at her age, fully know: that by being truthful and, yes, maybe cruel, but also gentle and rare, Sister Mary is now and always will be a beautiful, unparalleled model for how and why to love.

Retrieve

FRIDAY NIGHT and sleep just starting to creep in, Nenny hears Kat throw off her blankets and leave the room. Nenny remains quiet and still. She hears Kat knock on the big bedroom door, then hears muffled voices. First Kat and Mom, then Kat and Mom and Rick. This goes on for a long while, Nenny sitting up in bed, straining to hear, the blankets bunched around her knees—but their voices are too far and too low. It's eleven o'clock on a Friday night in June.

Finally, Kat returns and gets back into bed. She doesn't say a word. Then a series of sounds: the garage door opening downstairs, the engine of the van starting, the garage door closing again.

"Where are they going?" Nenny asks. She has to fight the urge to be terrified, straining against it like walking into a strong wind.

"To find Charles," Kat says bluntly, as if this isn't a majorly big deal.

"What?" What about the power of secrets? What about knowing what no one else knows? What about tyrannizing one another, hoarding one another's infractions and mistakes? "You told them?"

"Yes, I told them," Kat says, like *Of course I did*. As if it's the obvious thing to do, as if she hasn't been sitting on the information for months. "He can't just wander around all night. It isn't safe."

This—Kat, protective and worried and genuinely concerned—falls around Nenny like settling silt. She lies back down, and they're both silent in the dark. Eventually the sounds repeat themselves in reverse, only this time Nenny can hear Charles opening and closing his bedroom door.

It's never really clear where he goes. No one mentions it, and it becomes one of their untouched, untalked-about things. Years later, when it finally does occur to Nenny to ask, she and Charles are at a pasta joint in Riverside, the kind of place where the breadsticks are free.

"Hey, where were you sneaking out to anyways?"

"What?"

"At night. When we were kids and you used to sneak out."

"Oh," he says, like he's forgotten it was ever a thing. He twirls pasta around on his fork. "Nowhere, really. I just kind of walked around."

"I used to think you were going into the sewers. Playing with rats."

And he looks at her like she's the one who's wandered off, like she's the one who's far away. "I was definitely not playing with rats," he says and signals to the waiter for more breadsticks.

—⁂—

In the morning, Mom says, "Maybe we should do something fun today." She doesn't mention the midnight run, and neither does anyone else. It's like it never happened. Everyone looks at Rick. He's the gatekeeper of fun things. He decides at what temperature things will heat up, at what temperature they cool. He doesn't say anything, which Mom, almost expertly, takes for a yes.

"Where should we go?" she asks. She looks at them all around the table, but everyone just kind of shrugs.

But then Charles speaks up, and since he's hardly spoken in months, everyone stops and stares.

"How about the tar pits?" he says, bent over his plate.

"The what?" someone asks.

"The tar pits. In La Brea." He looks up then, that old look on his face, like he's dealing with a bunch of morons.

There's a pause while everyone lets this sink in—not the tar pits, but Charles, him, speaking, participating in what's happening in the room. It's like a strange wind has come in from some open door.

"I think that's a great idea," Rick finally says, and everyone nods, though who knows what they're agreeing to anymore.

In the Pit

THE LA Brea Tar Pits are not exactly aptly named, because it's really just one pit, singular, as far as Nenny can tell—a small lake of belching tar that smells as you'd expect it to smell, like a melty old road. Green bubbles burst through the rainbow oil surface, and the smell gets worse. At the far end is a sculpture of three woolly mammoths, one in the muck and two onshore, and the boys run down and twine their fingers through the fence, and Tiny whispers, "Coooool."

The truth is, Nenny does not now, nor will she ever, give two farts about fossils or dinosaurs. She tries, she really does, because Rick grimaces deep when it comes time to pay—it's almost sixty bucks—and Nenny knows how special this kind of thing is, this kind of treat. But when they go in and stand before the giant skeleton of a saber-toothed tiger, and everyone oohs and aahs, including Kat, all Nenny sees is a bunch of old bones. There's an elaborate timeline of humanity, from fish to ape to man, and a history of the tar pits, photos of animals long extinct, maps of landmass movements throughout time, placards detailing how ancient people lived, what the world was like then—how inhospitable, how cold—and none of it, not a word, sinks in.

Everyone else, every single member of her family, is completely engrossed, this suddenly the most captivating place they've ever been. Mom runs her fingers along the placards, as if trying to absorb every word, and Rick rocks back and forth on his heels while he reads. Tiny and Bubbles have their faces pressed to the glass room with the paleontologists inside—like lab-coated animals at a zoo—and Kat, even Kat, is snapping pictures left and right. After a while Nenny realizes that Charles is not around.

She finds him outside, on a little footbridge at the edge of the pit. He doesn't tell her to bug off, which must mean she can stay. The tar is as smooth as glass in some places, bubbling and puckered in others. She stands not far from Charles but not close either, and it occurs to her that maybe her disinterest arises in the face of such scale. What is a day, a month, next to a billion years? On the wall in the museum there'd been a painting of an astronaut, floating in space, among stars and then stars and then stars. In class they'd spent all that time on the size of the world, but not once had they stopped to consider the size of themselves.

Out of nowhere Charles says, "That's us."

Nenny turns. She'd nearly forgotten he was there. "What's us?"

"That," he says and points. "Buncha tar."

Nenny looks at the pit and thinks, *Maybe you, I'm not tar,* but knows what he means. What he means is his own answer to scale: that one day we'll return and return again, all of us bound for that same black soup. He leans over and, without ceremony or poetics, spits.

"Hey!" A security guard materializes out of nowhere, yelling. "No spitting!" He charges up the bridge's incline and stops with his hands on his hips. He looks like the kind of guy who wanted to be a cop but had to settle for this—bulging at the waist, a face as red as raw meat. Nenny knows she should be afraid of his barking, but honestly, she feels nothing at all.

"Sorry," Charles says, but there are real sorries and sorries like this, not even looking at the guy, accompanied by an indifferent shrug.

The guy looks at the back of Charles's head, then over at Nenny, then at Charles again, clearly weighing what to do. "Who are you with? Where's your mother?"

What happens then will never leave Nenny, not in a million years. Charles looks that stupid no-cop right in the eyes. "My mother's dead," he says, holding the man's gaze like clenching a fist. When the stupid guy starts to respond, Charles doesn't even give him a chance. He turns his head and snorks all his snot into his throat, then hocks a massive loogie right into the pit.

—✺—

"He said his mother was dead," No-Cop almost demands of Mom when everyone shows up. He'd sort of half dragged them into the office, like a scene in a cartoon, and made an announcement over the PA when Nenny finally revealed their names. Everyone is shocked when he says this—one, because it was said, and two, because now he repeats it? They all watch Mom.

"His mother *is* dead," she says, as matter-of-fact as Charles had been. This, too, is like something dropping to the floor. "I'm his stepmother."

No-Cop sort of coughs or clears his throat. "Well, I—"

"What exactly happened?" Rick interrupts.

"Your son, sir. He spit in the pit."

"He what?" Rick says, justifiably confused.

"The pit, sir. The lake? Your son spit in it." No-Cop sort of lifts then drops his hand. "And, well, spitting's not allowed."

Rick's face remains blank, and he looks around at all of them, as if for interpretation or help.

"He spit in the pit, *Dad*," Kat finally says, leaning on Charles's chair. Charles sits quietly with his hands on his lap.

"Yes, he spit in the pit, dear," Mom chimes in, a smile playing on her lips. Well, that's all it takes, for Mom to say it. They crowd this meat-faced wannabe cop out of his own stupid room.

"He spit in the pit," Bubbles says, grabbing Tiny by the shoulders and giving him a little shake. "He spit in the pit!"

Kat picks it up. "He spit, in the pit," like limbo, *How low, can you go?*

"He spit, in the pit! He spit, in the pit!" Bubbles and Tiny sing, swinging each other's hands. It's like in-your-face cha-cha-cha. Mom looks at Rick, moving her shoulders to the rhythm. She doesn't even look at the cop.

"Sir?" the cop says, as if pleading.

"Enough," Rick says to all of them, even Mom, and that's it—enough's enough. He looks at Charles, and Charles knows what to do.

"I'm sorry I spit in the pit," Charles says, his eyes on the floor.

"Well, all right. Don't let it happen—" But they're already halfway out the door. Nobody says anything. They trudge wordlessly to the car.

—⁓—

It's a two-hour drive home, most of which takes place in silence. It's impossible to tell if they've ruined a good day or, with their antics, defined one. A twisting tension fills the van, two-sided. On one side is the very real possibility that they're all in deep shit; on the other is a thing that is impossible to name but crystallizes the moment Rick does something he would otherwise never do, which is to roll down the window and spit. Everyone knows everyone else is smiling, though it's dark in the van. Somehow, in the midst of all this, because of all this, they've become something together, however choppy, however flawed: some kind of unit, some kind of tribe.

Passage

WEEKS GO by. Summer seeps in and with it the heat and the smog. It's so hot you could fry an egg, as the saying goes, and Peter Garcia from 6B proves it: raids his mother's fridge and absconds with half a dozen, sets to work on a patch of patio near the still-disgusting pool. The eggs crackle and pop like an effect from a space movie, like alien flesh cooking in a pan, and the Citrus Grove kids circle and watch those suckers fry. It is the first of July. On the Fourth, they walk down to the university parking lot, because Dad hates fighting for a spot on the grass. In the near distance you can hear the boys' choir singing "Battle Hymn of the Republic," as they do every year. The fireworks are standard-issue: breathtaking, beautiful, and totally indistinguishable from the ones last year or from the ones in years to come. "Daddy, what's a grape of wrap?" Tiny asks on the way home. He's holding a little flag someone gave him, waving it around. "A what?" Dad asks. "A grape of wrap," Tiny says, then sings, "He is stamping on the village where the grapes of wrap are stored!" Bubbles interrupts. "Wrath," he corrects. Maybe this is why they call him Bubbles—light as air, so light as to be imperceptible, but then what would they do without him? A few days later, Boots's aunt comes to visit and says what everyone's been thinking when she sees the pool: "Pathetic." Her name is Janine. She's tall and freckled with fire-red hair—nothing like Boots or her mother at all—and when Boots and Nenny tell her that, no, they don't know how to make friendship bracelets, she says, "What on earth do you mean?" and shows them how. Now it is their passion, their ritual, their religion—bracelets circle their ankles and arms, adorn their bedposts, spill from their shelves—and when they walk to Thrifty's to escape the heat, they skip the magazines and nail polish altogether and head straight for the thread. They spend hours in the aisle, poring over color combinations (gold with salmon and aquamarine, turquoise and mustard and dark chimney red), and afterward they each buy a single scoop of ice cream. By late July you can't even see the mountains anymore. Winter and spring are so clear you might reach out and touch them, but summers, the smog rolls in from LA and slumps over everything like a beast. Cosby starts to smell like baked cheese, and Joey the cat hides in the closet all day. Sometimes it's hard to even breathe. Bubbles rasps at his new inhaler and stays mostly indoors. One weekend Charles says, "Let me try," and swipes the plastic mouthpiece with his shirt before placing it between his lips. "Oh shit," he says, his voice pinched and strained. It's hard to tell from his reaction if it's the best thing or the worst thing or both, but when Mom catches them at it fifteen minutes later—Bubbles and Charles passing the inhaler back and forth, their faces giddy and splotched and red—she cries, "Are you insane?" and snatches it from their hands. It's so hot the asphalt reignites from last year, when crews shut down most of the neighborhood from Wabash to Dearborn. "Come look at this," Kat says and leads

Nenny to the curb at the corner. An assortment of tiny, remarkable things lies embedded in the street: a coil of metal and two house keys and a number of nuts and bolts. "Neat, huh?" Kat says and presses the toe of her shoe into the road, which gives like cooling wax. She pulls two pennies from her pocket and hands Nenny one. They stoop and together push their coins into the melting road. The asphalt folds over the coins' edges like pulling someone in for a hug, and there the pennies stay, months, years, still there now, even, which is another way of saying forever. (Someone should let Laura Hofstader, PhD, know: when someone dies, it sucks like hell, but it can also bring people closer together because sometimes a person who was a jerk isn't a jerk anymore.) At Dad's, Nenny lies across the kitchen floor because it's too hot even for carpet or couch or chairs. "Da-ad," she says, because sometimes it takes two syllables to make your point. "Could you ple-ease call Mr. Baldy and tell him to fix the po-ol?" It's the principle of the thing, dang it. Yes, the world is very big, but children everywhere—especially in this kind of oppressive heat—deserve at the very least a pool. Dad looks at her from the counter, where he's sorting mail. It's a look that doesn't need explaining. It's not unlike the look Mom wore when Windsor died. There's something gentle and hurting in a person's face when they tell you something no one wants to have to say. "Honey, I don't think Mr. Baldy is going to fix the pool." And that's it, those words are enough. From then on and for the next several weeks, each time Nenny sees Chuck Baldy it's as if it's for the first and final time: how he shuffles, pale and stooped, to the mailboxes and back again, bent and weak like an old man. Thing is, he's not that old. She gets a letter from Boots, who's with her grandmother in Arkansas. "Dear Nenny," the letter begins. "Do you like this paper? My grandma took me to a stationery store." It features drawings of a crocodile, sitting in a chaise longue and sipping lemonade. "Did I tell you about Bradley? He's my grandma's cat. He ran away after grandpa died, but now he's back. He has an extra digit on his paws." She's drawn a picture of him and labeled it "Bradley the Cat with Thumbs." She ends the letter "Love, Boots," with a postscript not to have any fun while she's gone. Nenny begins a response letter right away. She doesn't have any interesting stationery so settles for graph paper instead. "Dear Boots," she begins. "My dad thinks Mr. Baldy might die. He looks very sick. If you saw him, you probably would not recognize him. I asked my dad what's the matter, and he said it's cancer but he doesn't know which kind. Hopefully he won't die before you come back." But he does die before Boots comes back. One day some flowers appear, carnations in a vase at his door, and then another vase, and then two more, and that's how Nenny knows that Chuck Baldy is gone. September comes and, with it, school. It's the same parade of dorks and freaks. When Nenny sees Matty Souza, she thinks, *Oh yeah, Matty!* because she hasn't thought about him in months. She still loves him, she supposes, watching him play basketball with the other boys, but she feels different, as if summer has tamped down something explosive and left a stillness in its wake. The fourth-grade nun is Sister Constance, and she seems all right. She's certainly not as cruel as Timothy (who is, though?), but neither does she shine in the way Mary did. She's from Poland and says things like "Thanks be to the Lord!" for silly reasons, like finding extra chalk in her desk. The heat has begun to abate, if only a little. Now it is possible to breathe. Now a plaid uniform feels less like a death trap and more like what it is: an itchy old sack. One day Dad says, "There's someone I want you to meet," and leads them across the parking lot after school. This day was bound to come. People live their lives, they slip and they fall and then they pick themselves up and live new ones. Even Nenny knows this. Previously she might've thought this would be a big deal—Dad holding her hand as he leads them to meet his new girlfriend—but it's not. The woman is cheerful and easygoing. "Hi, everyone," she says with a sweet smile, and where Dad met her and when exactly they have time to go out is beside the point. The point is she seems nice and not phony at all, and she doesn't even flinch when they go to Denny's and Tiny spills his Coke all over the table. She just says, "Whoops," and helps clean it up. Her name is Rhonda, and soon she is a regular fixture in their lives. Most nights, it seems, she's coming over to make casserole or chili or stew from scratch, and stays after dinner to read them stories before they shuffle off to bed. Autumn settles in. The crepe myrtles take on the skeletal look they'll hold through winter and into spring. Leaves fill the gutters and sidewalks; the sun begins to feel that much farther away. The smog clears, and at night, finally, you can see the stars. Mom's friend at the hospital is a nurse but also a budding stylist, and she comes over one Saturday with a little bag filled with scissors and combs. Her name is Cheryl. She sets up a chair on the back patio and whips a bib around Mom's shoulders, just like in a salon, and starts spraying Mom's hair with a squirt bottle. She must have eyes in the back of her head, buried in her mounds of curls, because she calls, "Come on out here, sugar," to Nenny, who's been watching from the window. Nenny goes outside, and Cheryl says, "Don't be shy. Pull up a chair." She's brash and graceful at once. Mom's got her head tipped forward like a woman in prayer, the way you do when someone trims your neck. Cheryl says, "You wanna be next?" and

Nenny shrugs. "We'll give you some cute little bangs." And then it's quiet for a long time, Cheryl hard at work and Mom with her eyes closed, leaves drifting across the pool in the early autumn breeze, and the way Cheryl cuts, gently taking locks of Mom's hair between her fingers and cutting, unhurried, just so, it's clear that Mom's told her everything, Windsor and Gabe and all the rest, things she's told no one else because who is there to tell? When Cheryl says, "I bet it'll be nice to have your mama back, huh?" Nenny's suspicions are confirmed, and her love for this woman is immediate and bright. The next day, Mom grabs her gardening gloves and her straw hat and steps into the yard. It hasn't been touched in months. All the flowers they planted last year are long dead, disintegrated to near dust, and everything, once again, is covered with weeds. A thick layer of leaves and dead bugs floats in the pool, and the stump that Rick found is still embedded in the hill, like a hunched shoulder poking through the earth. Mom sighs and pulls on her gloves. She goes to the corner where Bubbles found his geode—or anyway his rock—and, through the window, Nenny watches as she digs. It is October and everything is quiet, except for the occasional sound of chimes blowing in the breeze. Every Sunday for the last few months Gramma Sadie has come to get Kat and Charles, and together the three of them go to put flowers on Windsor's grave. This is a new ritual, maybe because lasting rituals take some time to emerge. Just then Nenny sees Mom sit up and with her fingers lift something out of the dirt, something that even from here you can see is melted and deformed—and there it is, there's that pot Chester buried in the yard. Two weeks later, there's a massive earthquake in the northern part of the state, and all of Nenny's fear comes rushing back. Fear is such a lonely place. It is a place impossible to describe, where the only known, certain thing is that we are all going to die. That night she lies awake, curled beneath the sheets, her mind a fractured thing. But Mom is an angel or a psychic or an empath or something else, something otherworldly, because she knows without words and in the morning says, "Come here," and pulls Nenny close. She's at the kitchen table, just as she is every morning, reading the paper in her robe. She hugs Nenny to her side, halfway onto her lap, and opens the paper to the middle. It's a two-page photo feature of the havoc the earthquake has wrought: entire buildings crushed like cakes, libraries and offices completely trashed, homes reduced to little more than piles of splintered wood. Most incredible and horrifying of all is a bridge that collapsed in the quake, the top tier snapping into pieces and smashing down onto the tier below. Mom does something then that no one else would do, because it would not occur to anyone else: she folds the edges of the paper down over the pictures until there's only one earthquake photo left. In it, a man—not a cop, not a firefighter, just a man—lies on his stomach at the edge of the collapsed portion of the bridge, his arms outstretched and reaching down. On the level below him, standing atop a half-crushed car, is a woman with her own arms raised, reaching back. If you think for one minute *How does that help? Showing pictures like that to a frightened child?* and you can't even see what really matters, what happens between the collapse and the folds, then you're an idiot anyways and you don't deserve to know. Out goes the fearful tide. The next day they drive—as a family, in the van—to San Bernardino. They haven't been to San Bernardino in months, not since Gramma B died. They're going to the rental house; they call it the Beech Street house because that's where it is. The Beech Street house is a sort of phantom thing in their lives, a nonentity that exists only once every few months, when the tenants forget to pay rent or Rick goes to fix a sprinkler or repair a fence post. But the renters moved out and now it's time to "just sell the damn thing and move on." So on Sunday they pile into the van and go for a drive. It's a short drive but a dismal one. Orange groves and tract homes give way to rocks and then more rocks, then dirt and freeways and houses that look as though they've been punched. "Looks like hell," Rick says of the neighborhood, and he's right: broken fences and overflowing garbage bins and junk in all the yards. Everyone is quiet, because here's the thing: this is more than just a weekend drive. The Beech Street house was the first house that Rick and Windsor and Charles and Kat, all four of them, ever lived in—Charles just a baby, Kat seven or eight years old—and everyone knows that, so this is a big deal. As with all big deals around here, they talk about and look at other things but never directly at the thing itself. The Beech Street house is a piece of crap. The front yard, yellow with dead weeds, is strewn with debris like the aftereffects of some war. The paint is peeled and cracked like an old man's skin, curling from the house as though reaching for something. Rick parks and everyone gets out of the van. Nenny looks up at the sky. Thick, churning clouds like overturned earth roll in a breeze too high to feel. Down here the air is still and nothing moves. The chain-link whines as Rick pushes open the fence, and they file quietly behind him. No one says anything, not even Tiny, who shuffles along holding Mom's hand. Rick reaches into his pocket, then stops halfway up the walk, tries another pocket, then a third. "Mother of shit," he says, and they all look at one another in surprise. "What's the matter?" Mom says, because this is supposed to be ceremonial, this whole thing, even if no one said so, and you really shouldn't say "Mother of shit" during ceremonial times. "I forgot the goddamn key," he shouts, and they all stand motionless in the afternoon light. Rick is not the kind of man to forget things, let alone something as important as a key. Rick curses under his breath, and Mom says, "All right," like *Come on, it's not the end of the world*. Charles picks up rocks and starts throwing them one by one, like angry missiles, down into the dust. It's sort of unclear why they're still here, locked out, milling about in the weed-blown yard. It seems like what should come next is fairly obvious: pile into the van and fight the whole way home. But then Kat—slowly, as if under a spell—goes up the walkway and puts her face to the dirty little window in the front door. Everyone slowly follows, making their way up the walk. There's a big picture window in the living room, and though the window is filthy, you can still see inside. The living room is dim and empty, orange carpet the color of mildew stretching from wall to wall. Nenny realizes she'd been expecting something else, strewn diapers or stained walls or something creepy and disturbed, like an animal carcass rotting in a corner, buzzing with flies. But it's empty and clean. "Mommy, whose house is this?" Tiny whispers, and Mom whispers back, "This is where Kat and Charles used to live." Nenny can't help but glance over at Rick. The night they returned from Uncle Max's, the night Windsor died, was a horrible, lonely night. They came home, and there was Charles in his shell and Kat crying upstairs, and after some time—minutes or hours, it's impossible to say—Tiny fell asleep on the floor so Mom said they should all go to bed. Nenny doesn't remember falling asleep, but she does remember waking up, a moment so small it could fit in a real moment's hand, when everything felt normal, everything felt fine—but then she saw the rise and fall of Kat's back, the rhythm of her breathing in the dark, and she remembered again, like being slapped, that nothing was normal, nothing was fine at all. The clock said 4 a.m. She got out of bed and wandered down the hall, haltingly, as if in a dream, hoping vaguely that Mom would wake up and hold her on the couch while she brushed her hair—but stopped short on the bottom step. Rick was standing in the kitchen, barefoot and in pajamas, staring out the window and sipping from a mug. Rick doesn't drink except for wine, partly because he can't stand the taste and partly, mostly, because his father was a mean and miserable man, a man so consumed by rage and addiction that he'd drink perfume and rubbing alcohol when the booze was gone. But something about the way Rick stood there, his glasses on at 4 a.m., unaware of her presence behind him (though he'd been in Vietnam), methodically raising the cup to his lips, over and over, told Nenny it wasn't coffee in that mug. A terrible thing is like a room in a house—you go in, you close a door, before you know it you're there all day—and Rick was as much in that room then as he is now, standing in front of the Beech Street house as if alone, peering through the glass. It occurs to Nenny, peripherally, like someone dropping something small in the far reaches of her brain, that he didn't actually forget the key—that he knows exactly where it is. Years from now, when Nenny and Charles and the boys are practically grown and Kat has moved out, they'll be sitting at the dinner table like they do every night when, out of nowhere, Tiny (who by then goes by his real name, not Tiny anymore) asks, "Hey, Rick, you ever kill anyone in Vietnam?" Loudly smacking his food, a false air of casualness to his words. Mom will get a look on her face as though someone has opened and then closed a door. Rick won't even look up from his plate, will just calmly say, "I shot at people but never had any kills," sipping then setting down his wine. Some information arrives wholly formed, like a package laid neatly in your lap, and when Rick answers Tiny's question, a number of things become immediately and immensely clear. The first is that everyone, not just Nenny, has circled and fixated on this for their entire lives, even Mom. The second is that Rick knows this, knows the enormity of it, how some things will keep you up at night—which leads to the third thing, which is that he's probably lying, telling them what they need to hear so that something can remain intact. Some lies are acts of deceit; others, acts of preservation and love. They drive home from the Beech Street house in silence, and the next day it starts to rain. Great, torrential sheets pour from the sky, silver like a tarnished mirror. Water swirls in churning eddies in the streets, gushes down the sidewalks and off roofs. At school, the classroom smells dank and sweaty, the particular stench of damp children shut indoors. "Cats and dogs," Dad says when he picks them up, wiping mist from the windshield with the back of his sleeve. In the afternoons, fat, unholy worms wriggle in the wet beside the pool, and Nenny and Boots stand on the balcony under umbrellas, watching Tiny finger-pinch worms and drop them into a jar. "Your brother's gross," Boots says, more in admiration than disgust, and Nenny agrees. The new superintendent's name is Mrs. Landry, and she's okay. She's already arranged for someone to clean the pool—they installed a replacement pump, skimmed the surface of leaves and dead flies—but it's not the same. Before, with Mr. Baldy, they had a purpose, a cause, and now that the pool is clean they don't have one anymore. The rain keeps falling and whatever you've heard, it all applies: the angels are peeing, God is crying, he's watering his lawn. "In Texas they call this a 'frog strangler,'" Bubbles says, and who knew he knew such a thing or why he knows it. During recess everyone stands under the eaves. Steve Smoot tips his head back and drinks the water streaming from the roof. "That's a good way to get diarrhea," Jackie Monroe notes, and everyone stares at her, because though probably accurate, it's still a gross thing to say. It's true that a storm like this would normally send Nenny into a panic, flood her with images of cars careening off the roads, everyone swept away—but strangely, it doesn't. It's a rain so strong and full there's no room to be scared, only quiet with awe. On Tuesday it rains and on Wednesday it rains and on Thursday it's raining still. Thursday night, Dad decides to make lasagna because Rhonda's coming over and he aims to impress. Other things too: He doesn't leave his underwear on the bathroom floor anymore, and every night he makes sure they brush their teeth. In the mornings he folds his sheets and blankets and stores them neatly under the couch, and he has taken to lighting a match after he poops as a courtesy to them all, which is something he never remembered to do before. All proof, one supposes, that love is powerful. Nenny wonders if this is what Dad was like when he met Mom—courteous and attentive and not wandering the land of his own distant thoughts. This dad is easy to love, because through his gestures, however small, it's like he's returned from some long trip and you know that he loves you back. Nenny and the boys are sprawled in the living room while Dad remembers how to cook. Bubbles has a notebook in his lap, Tiny's on his stomach on the floor, his legs triangled behind him, drawing little people with crayons. It's *Fantasy Island* on TV, which is a show that nobody likes, so the volume's low. And anyway, Nenny's got a new book that Boots lent her. It's called *Starring Sally J. Freedman as Herself,* and it's nothing like the Baby-Sitters Club. The Baby-Sitters Club is about, well, a bunch of babysitters, while this one is about a girl and her family, and also about the size of the world. The news comes on, and Dad says, "Turn it up," so Bubbles does. "The sun rose this morning on a Germany where everyone can travel at will," Tom Brokaw says. Tom Brokaw has the grainy voice of a frog, like it stuck halfway when he was clearing his throat. He's wearing gloves and a thick coat, standing in front of a big crowd of cheering people. Dad comes around the counter. "Turn it up! Turn it up!" he says, and Bubbles says, "I already did," and Dad says, "Turn it up again!" and Bubbles makes a face like *Geez Louise* but does. "The sound that you hear and what you're seeing tonight," Tom Brokaw says, rather poetically, "not hammers and sickles but hammers and chisels, as young people take down this wall"—he pauses dramatically—"bit by bit." Dad stands motionless by the couch, his mouth hanging open. He stays like that for a full minute, then says, "That's incredible. This is incredible." He's wearing oven mitts. Nenny and the boys look at one another and kind of shrug. On TV, people are dancing and chanting in the streets, waving around bottles of champagne and things like hammers and other tools. "I've got to call Rhonda," Dad says, looking around wildly for the phone even though it's always on the wall right there. "Rhonda!" he practically shouts. "They're tearing down the wall!" Which is a weird thing to phone-yell at your girlfriend. There's a pause. "The wall," Dad says. "The Berlin Wall." There's another pause while he listens. "Yeah, okay. See you at six." He listens some more. "Sure, Jell-O is fine. Jell-O's great, hon," and hangs up. He comes back looking a little deflated but stands again by the side of the couch. A series of images plays on the screen: soldiers straddling the giant wall, striking it with picks; people foot-boosting one another up and helping each other from falling down; an old newsreel clip shows a woman weeping into a handkerchief while soldiers drag another woman away. "Daddy, what's a berling wall?" Tiny asks from the floor. Dad doesn't answer right away, just stands by the couch incredulously shaking his head. "Dad?" Bubbles asks again, and when Dad answers, he says, "It's been there a really long time," which is not an answer at all. Who knows what any of it means, but clearly it's a big deal. Maybe Dad will scrap the lasagna and take them to McDonald's instead. Nenny thinks of Sister Mary, wonders if she's also watching the news, wonders if a nun's house even has a TV. She sees Mary frequently in the halls at school, and when Nenny waves, however sheepishly, Mary always waves back. She watches Mary's new class line up and wonders if they know yet about the size of the world, or if that comes later, if that's a second-half-of-the-year kind of thing. On the TV, strangers embrace, tears streaming down their cheeks. Next week Sister Constance's brother, who lives in West Berlin, will wrap up and box a chunk of discarded wall the size of a fist, and it will travel first by car and then by train and then by air and then likely by train again to arrive, somewhat miraculously, at Sacred Heart, where Sister Constance will stand at the front of the class and try her best not to cry. Now Nenny sits in the living room with Tiny and Bubbles and Dad, hoping secretly that the lasagna will burn, rain trickling outside, a rare euphoria being broadcast on the screen, and thinks about Mary, thinks about God—God as Tom Brokaw with his gravelly voice, God as that woman crying, that soldier with the pickax, or that man, some random guy, just reaching up and grabbing pieces of the wall, using his own bare hands to tear it down.

Acknowledgments

I am here to dispel the notion that writers succeed on their own. It's a lie! I owe so much to so many.

Thank you, first and foremost, to Chris Clemans. Your brilliance is blinding, your insight is incredible, and your humor is unmatched. I am beyond thrilled to know you and to work with you.

Thank you to Carina Guiterman, for your genius and your enthusiasm. You have made this a much, much better book.

Amber Cady: I love you, my sparkling dark matter. Leslie Outhier: I want to giggle and draw with you forever. Tamara Taylor: you are my heart-shaped rock.

Special thanks to Andy Elliott, who's a master at the crossword and cleaning out the fridge. And to Dean and Jeff and all the kids, for always making me feel loved.

Big heartfelt thanks to these incredible gems: Bill Clegg, Peter Orner, Tupelo Hassman, Matthew Clark Davison, Tavia Stewart, Ryan Bartlett, Dustin Heron, Jacob Evans, Neale Jones, the Minninghams, Paquita Schoellhorn and the entire Outhier clan, Doug and Kaye Sharon, Windsor Meyer, James Chan, James Dirito, Shaun and Molly Winter, Ben Ricker, Jillian Drewes, Nancy Espinoza Magana and Josema Zamorano,

Jenga Keenan, Ali Schneider, and Aristotle Johns. Extra-special thanks to Bryan Steelman and the whole PQN clan.

I am deeply indebted to the MacDowell Colony and to the many lovely artists I met while there. Special thanks to Zack Zadek, for keeping me on task and then serenading me afterward.

Thank you also to Amanda Brower, for your early enthusiasm for this book.

I would be nothing without my family. They are a wild and weird and wonderful bunch. Thank you especially to Cassie and Chris, for your grace and encouragement throughout this whole thing.

Of course, the most important thank-yous are the most difficult to write. Tucker, thank you for years of encouragement, adventures, laughs, and love. Your name is forever inscribed on my squishy little heart.